A
Reputation
Dies

A Reputation Dies

ALICE CHETWYND LEY

St. Martin's Press
New York

Library of Congress Cataloging in Publication Data

Ley, Alice Chetwynd.
    A reputation dies.

    I. Title.
PR6062.E965R4   1985   823'.914   84-18313
ISBN 0-312-67574-7

First published in Great Britain by Methuen London Ltd.

10 9 8 7 6 5 4 3 2

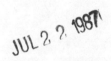

'At ev'ry word a reputation dies.'

Alexander Pope
The Rape of the Lock

A
Reputation
Dies

CHAPTER I

*L*ady Windlesham, like many another fashionable London hostess, wished her soirées to be considered more eventful than the general run of such affairs. But even she would not have desired anything so eventful as a murder.

The London season of 1816 had scarcely begun, so it was highly unlikely that her entertainment would earn the accolade of being 'a sad crush'. Nevertheless, quite a few eminent members of the *ton* were to be present. The guests were nearly all acquainted with each other, of course, as Town society consisted of a small, select circle meeting frequently at the same fashionable gatherings. The only new face, she reflected, would be Lord Velmond's young bride, a girl from Somerset.

She congratulated herself on having secured Mr Marmaduke Yarnton. He was much in demand; not because anyone liked the man, but his fund of malicious gossip and innuendo seldom failed to amuse a coterie avid for scandal. Mr Yarnton did not specialize in the larger scandals, such as the amours of Lord Byron which were at present being exclaimed over in the drawing-rooms and providing heaven-sent material for the print shop caricaturists. Instead he contented himself with humbler matters, which he ferreted out painstakingly by keeping a watchful eye on his acquaintance. A word dropped here, a look there, would intrigue the curious and sting the guilty, lending a welcome astringent touch to an otherwise conventional gathering.

Among the early guests to arrive were Lord and Lady Velmond, the newly-weds.

'So good of you to come,' fluted Lady Windlesham.

'Not at all, ma'am – good of you to invite us,' replied Velmond, a personable young man in his early thirties, with brown hair swept into a fashionable Brutus style and clear, honest blue eyes. 'Don't believe you've met my wife? Lucy, Lady Windlesham.'

Lucilla Velmond curtseyed while her hostess studied her. Not a day over nineteen and as pretty as report had promised. Pale gold hair framing a roses and cream complexion, a slender figure well set off by a discreetly décolleté gown of primrose silk, and the most unusual amber-coloured eyes. It was not so surprising that the wealthy young peer for whom the Town's matchmaking mamas had been on the catch for years, should have fallen victim to the charms of a penniless country girl. But such a girl as this!

Oddly, though, the chit did not look too happy, as Lady Quainton, an old acquaintance, remarked later to her hostess.

'There seems a little constraint between our lovebirds, wouldn't you say, Maria? The child looks too pale and fine-drawn. Undoubtedly it's a lovematch on Velmond's side, for why else should a man in his position take a dowerless bride from the depths of the country? But possibly she may have been persuaded into it against her inclination, for I hear her father and brother are quite done up. There may have been another young man in her own neighbourhood whom she'd have preferred. Though what girl in her senses would pass over such a handsome beau as Velmond for anyone else is more than I can comprehend!'

Lady Windlesham, who still had an eye for a personable gentleman, agreed.

Mr Henry Cleveland, MP and his wife Sophia had been quarrelling in the carriage on their way to the soirée. Mrs Cleveland was complaining bitterly about the retrenchments which had been made lately in their household affairs.

'Why you should find it necessary to sell off half the cattle in your stables and reduce the numbers of indoor servants, I cannot at all understand!' she snapped, with a toss of her expensively coiffed dark head which set the diamond drops in her ears glittering. 'We can't possibly be as purse-pinched as that!'

'Can we not?' he asked sardonically. 'When your bureau drawer is stuffed as full as it can be with bills for gowns, pelisses and God knows what other items of female attire, enough to last you should you live to be an octogenarian! And not one of the damned things for less than a hundred guineas!'

She stared at him coldly. 'Do you suppose I should patronize the linen draper's and make up my own gowns? As the wife of a member of His Majesty's Government I've a certain standard to maintain, you'll allow. Besides, when has anyone worried over a few unpaid bills? You used not to be so – so clutch-fisted as you've become this past twelvemonth! I'm sure I'm at my wits' end to account for it – unless,' she added, spitefully, 'it's because you're at that time of life when a man feels a certain malaise. Perhaps you should consult Dr Wetherby to see if a little blood-letting cannot cure you of these absurd megrims. I dare say he'll be at Maria Windlesham's this evening, so you can mention it to him.'

Although in general doctors were considered to be on a social level with tradesmen, and therefore unlikely to be invited to *ton* parties, Dr Ralph Wetherby was, like the Prince Regent's Sir William Knighton, an exception to the rule. He had built up a fashionable practice and a consequently affluent standard of living, so was everywhere received.

Cleveland snorted. 'Wetherby! I only wish it might be as simple as that. I tell you, Sophia, I'm rapidly going under the hatches and unless I can find a way – but, God, what's the use of trying to explain?'

'I can only suppose you've been gaming,' she replied with an impatient shrug, 'though I must admit that I never realized deep play was among your vices. However, no doubt you'll come about before long with Roderick's assistance. If you take my advice you'll leave all your business affairs in his capable hands – he's uncommon shrewd. Meantime, for pity's sake let's have no more of this unseemly pinching and scraping! I declare I'm quite worn down by it!'

'You were not always so pleased with Peyton,' retorted Cleveland. 'After Cecilia came home from school I recall that for a time you urged me to get rid of him, even though it was at your insistence that I employed him in the first place.'

'Yes, well, that was because they began to be on far too easy terms for my liking and I was afraid she might become attached to him – or fancy herself so! – as he's a prodigiously personable young man and she was at an impressionable age. But I spoke to her seriously on the subject and fortunately she's a sensible girl and quite saw that it would not do. Then it wasn't long before her come-out when she met plenty of more eligible bachelors to give her thoughts a new direction and quickly contracted a very good match. So *that* objection to him is long past, and we may indeed be thankful that you've obtained such an excellent secretary at what can only be considered a most reasonable salary, even by your present penny-pinching standards!'

Roderick Peyton was a talented young man with an ambition eventually to enter Parliament himself. His family were in reduced circumstances, so on his coming down from Cambridge nearly three years before he had been obliged to look about him for a means of earning a living. It chanced that Sophia Cleveland was very distantly related to Peyton's mother, and an over-zealous cousin, always eager to promote the interests of even the remotest branches of her family, had nagged at Cousin Sophia until she had persuaded her husband to employ the luckless young man.

Cleveland made no reply to all this but passed a weary hand over his brow. There was never any point in arguing with his wife, as long experience had taught him.

Presently their carriage pulled up outside Lady Windlesham's house, ablaze with lights and with two liveried footmen waiting at the top of the carpeted steps. The occupants of the chaise dismounted, schooling their expressions into something more nearly approaching the degree of cordiality expected of guests arriving for an evening's entertainment.

Eventually they entered the drawing-room, an elegant apartment in eau-de-nil and gold, already filled with chattering groups. Waiters circulated with liquid refreshment. Sophia Cleveland looked about her, noting which females of her acquaintance were wearing the same gown she had observed on a previous occasion and similar matters which might provide tit-bits of gossip. But she soon saw that she would be outdone;

for among the groups moved Mr Yarnton, a mincing figure in formal evening dress, dropping his poisoned barbs with a cynical twist of his thin lips. Usually a ripple of laughter greeted his remarks, for he had a clever tongue and most people were only too ready to laugh at the follies of others. Some, however, had no taste for his style of witticism and turned contemptuously away at his approach.

Beau Brummel made a late entrance, as usual. Lady Windlesham had hesitated over sending him an invitation as his circumstances were now greatly changed. He had quarrelled with the Prince Regent some time since and was so deeply in debt that it was rumoured he would be obliged to run from his creditors any day. None of this showed, however, in his elegant appearance and cool manner. Having conferred the honour of his presence on the assembly, he left within twenty minutes, but not before Yarnton had managed to administer one of his stings.

'I wonder,' he asked of the small group surrounding the Beau, 'who will advise Prinney on the cut of his coats *now*?'

Smiles were hastily concealed. Everyone knew that before the quarrel the Regent had often consulted Brummell on sartorial matters. If Yarnton had hoped to take a rise out of the erstwhile leader of fashion, he was to be disappointed. Brummell elevated his nose as if he had detected a particularly bad smell and continued his desultory conversation with those about him. He departed soon afterwards and Yarnton moved to another part of the room.

'Must admit,' remarked a man in the group with a chuckle, 'that chap Yarnton's devilish amusin', what? Always hits the nail on the head, don't y'know.'

'Aye, and one of these days I shouldn't wonder if he's hit on the head himself,' replied another. 'Like a demned wasp – needs swatting.'

'Oh, no, don't suppose anyone takes him seriously enough for that. Of course one can't like the fellow, exactly, but he does provide a little light relief at these affairs, what?'

Lady Quainton had been joined by Lady Kinver, a widow of

her own age whom she had known for many years. It did not escape Lady Quainton's sharp eye that her friend looked a trifle peaky; but she wisely refrained from commenting on this, knowing that such remarks, however sympathetic, only made one feel worse.

They exchanged family news for some time until they became drawn into a group consisting of the Clevelands, the Velmonds, a friend of Lord Velmond's named William Bradfield, and Dr Wetherby. The gentlemen soon began talking together on male topics, leaving the ladies to chat among themselves.

Mrs Cleveland was a compulsive talker and the part required of the others was slight enough for Lady Quainton to leave the responses to her friend Lady Kinver after a time, so that she herself might concentrate on drawing out Lucilla Velmond. So far the young bride had scarcely uttered a word.

'Is this your first time in Town, Lady Velmond?' she began, although she knew the answer.

'Yes, ma'am,' responded Lucy shyly.

'Then you may find it a little trying at first, although you'll soon grow accustomed. I dare say you frequently attended the assemblies in Bath, for I collect your home was near the town?'

Lucy shook her head. 'No, ma'am, I have been very little used to going into company, I fear. There was no one to chaperone me. My mother died when I was a child and I have no sisters.'

Lady Quainton raised her brows in surprise.

'But surely your father arranged for some older female companion for you?' she asked mildly.

Lucy hesitated. 'My aunt, papa's sister, manages the household. But she does not care for any kind of entertainment, except to provide dinners now and then for papa's friends.'

'Dear me, that sounds a dull life for a young girl! Still, doubtless you will make up for it now that you are married and living in Town.'

'Yes,' agreed Lucy in a doubtful tone.

Lady Quainton laughed. 'Oh, pray don't be put off by the fact that you find yourself surrounded almost entirely by dowagers this evening! Once the season's in full swing you will meet some of the younger set and soon find friends of your own age.'

Lucy's face brightened. 'I did meet a young lady the other day whom I liked extremely,' she said with more animation 'She came to call on us with her parents, Viscount and Lady Rutherford. She is much about my own age. Are you at all acquainted with her, Lady Quainton?'

'Anthea Rutherford, indeed I am! She's an engaging puss, full of fun and gig! I've been intimate with the whole family for a very long time. The late Lady Rutherford – Anthea's grandmother, you know – was a girlhood friend of mine. Her eldest son now holds the title. She had six offspring altogether but my favourite is the youngest, my godson, Justin. You may have heard your husband speak of him, for they were up at Oxford together and have remained close friends ever since.'

'Oh, yes, I have, ma'am. My husband –' she coloured faintly at the words, somewhat to Lady Quainton's amusement – 'tells me that it is some time since he saw Mr Rutherford. It seems that the gentleman is out of England at present.'

Lady Quainton chuckled. 'One never quite knows where Justin will be or what he'll be at! He may be deep in research in the Oxford libraries – he's quite a scholar and has published a book on the architectural antiquities of Greece – or else grubbing around his dusty old ruins and generally poking his nose into trouble. Especially the latter! He's not at all like the general run of academics. Every now and then he feels an urge to take himself out of his books and plunge into some adventure or other. The last was when he acted as an intelligence officer for Wellington during the Peninsular campaign. He says he suffers from a consuming curiosity which now and then breaks out in unexpected directions. His family don't quite know what to make of him – all except Anthea, that's to say. She's a good deal like him herself and frankly adores him! So absurd, don't you think, a girl of nineteen with an uncle of three and thirty? But such oddities occur in large families.'

Lucy, who had listened fascinated to this account, smiled.

'You sound very fond of him yourself, ma'am.'

'Why, so I am. I've no son of my own, you know, and I'm his godmother.'

She broke off and looked up as a young man approached Mr Cleveland diffidently, evidently wishing to have a private word with him.

'That's young Peyton, Cleveland's secretary,' she informed Lucy in an undertone. 'Do you not think him handsome, my dear?'

Lucy studied the newcomer covertly. He was in his middle twenties, slender and fair-haired, with a classical cast of countenance. She was unwilling to think any man as handsome as her husband, but grudgingly nodded.

He and Cleveland drew a little apart, conversing rapidly in undertones.

A mellifluous voice broke in upon the conversation of the four female members of the group.

'Ah, my dear ladies, so far I have not had the pleasure of speaking with you, alas!'

It was Yarnton who had joined them in his usual soft-footed manner. He bowed to each in turn, naming them as he did so.

'Delightful to see you all in such bloom,' he purred. 'It is more than can be said of some ladies present, I fear. Do you suppose that Mrs Crathorne intends her hair to look so very – roseate – or is it an error made by an over-enthusiastic coiffeur? I cannot think it an improvement, can you, dear Mrs Cleveland? And your own coiffure such a perfect shade of black.'

Sophia Cleveland flushed. She liked to think her artistic touches undetectable. But she was not going to give this man the satisfaction of knowing that he had piqued her, so she tittered dutifully at Mrs Crathorne's expense.

Yarnton moved farther into the circle, bowing in the direction of the gentlemen. They all responded correctly but without enthusiasm. Cleveland had finished his short conference with his secretary and the latter was just about to turn away. He hesitated a moment as Yarnton spoke.

'Matters of importance, gentlemen?' asked Yarnton with raised eyebrows. 'And at a soirée? But there, life is full of mysteries, is it not? One in particular has been exercizing my mind a good deal of late. Pray can any of you . . . ' – he let his cynical glance travel round the entire group – 'enlighten me as to who Mr Thompson may be?'

Lady Quainton, her besetting sin of curiosity at once to the fore, cast a shrewd eye over her companions. Lady Kinver, who was next to her, gave a nervous start. Lucy turned pale and surely Cleveland had momentarily registered a quickly suppressed reaction? The others frowned in what appeared to be bewilderment.

'Well, who the deuce *is* he?' demanded Velmond. 'I for one never heard of the fellow. Come on, Yarnton, you may as well explain. This is another of your little jests, ain't it?'

Yarnton shook his head, continuing to study them with a cynical eye.

'Lord Velmond is quite right,' put in Dr Wetherby in a pedantic tone. 'If this is intended to be amusing, you will need to explain further before we can appreciate the humour of it.'

'Alas, there are reasons why I cannot do so, my dear doctor. Yet I believe the gentleman in question is among us this evening, perhaps not so *very* far away?'

'Thompson, Thompson,' – Lady Quainton repeated the name, her eyes alert. 'I can think of no one belonging to our circle with that name, although doubtless it's common enough.'

'Where did you hear it, and in what circumstances?' demanded Cleveland, suddenly.

'Oh, dear me, to reveal that would spoil everything,' replied Yarnton, plaintively. 'But I see you cannot, or will not, help me, so I'll take my leave of you for the present. Your servant, ladies – gentlemen.'

'And good riddance,' said Velmond, *sotto voce*, as he moved towards his wife. 'Lucy, are you feeling the heat? You look a trifle unwell.'

'Oh, no, no, I'm perfectly all right,' she replied hurriedly. 'That is – perhaps I will just go to the ladies' retiring-room and bathe my face. It is rather hot in here.'

'I'll come with you,' offered Lady Quainton.

'No, pray don't trouble, ma'am, I'll only be gone a moment.'

She walked quickly away. She was followed presently by Lady Kinver and soon afterwards the group dispersed, drifting to join other acquaintances in the room. Only Lady Quainton remained, seated on a gilt chair which combined elegance with discomfort, brooding over what had just passed.

Her reverie was interrupted by the sudden reappearance of Mr Yarnton, who bent confidentially over her chair.

'You look pensive, dear lady, and who can wonder at it. One's acquaintances are so amusing, are they not? They foolishly suppose that their little foibles and follies go unnoticed, but I fancy you are one of the few who, like myself, make it your business to observe your fellow creatures.'

'If I do, sir,' retorted Lady Quainton tartly, 'I hope it is with compassion!'

He spread his hands. 'But of course! One had only to see the kindly way in which you were drawing out dear Lady Velmond earlier on to realize how *pure* were your motives. And there must be a vast deal of interest to discover in that quarter. For instance, I saw the young bride myself the other day, alighting from a hackney carriage – a *hackney*, mark you! – in a most unfashionable spot, a street near Petticoat Lane. And heavily veiled, at that, though I did not fail to recognize her. One wonders – '

He was seized suddenly in a remorseless grip and twisted round. Lord Velmond's furious countenance thrust itself at him.

'Did I hear the name of *my wife* on your scurrilous tongue?'

Yarnton passed his tongue over his dry lips but did his best to keep calm.

'You mistake, my lord,' he stuttered. 'A private conversation with Lady Quainton. . . . You have no right – '

Velmond shook him as a terrier shakes a rat.

'No right! Who has a better right, you – you – '

His voice had risen, and those standing nearby turned to stare in shocked surprise. Lucy had just re-entered the room and now came running forward. She took Velmond's arm.

'George – no, please! Don't, I beg you, make a scene – pray come away!'

He shook her off impatiently; but others were now hurrying to the spot, among them Dr Wetherby and Bradfield. The doctor, a well-built man, pulled Velmond off his victim and firmly restrained him from making a further attack.

'Don't be a damned fool, my lord,' he said in a quiet voice

that carried authority. 'Can't make a scene in Lady Windlesham's drawing-room. Not a gentlemanly thing to do. Besides, think of your wife, you won't wish to involve her in a scandal.'

Cleveland, who had also come quickly forward, signed to Yarnton to make himself scarce, a hint which the other was not slow in taking. His instincts of self-preservation were well developed. Once he had gone Velmond relaxed and freed himself from the doctor's grasp.

'Suppose you're right,' he admitted, grudgingly, 'but I tell you, Wetherby, I'd dearly love to give that scoundrel a sound thrashing, damme if I wouldn't!'

'No doubt, no doubt,' agreed Dr Wetherby in a soothing tone. 'But anything of the kind is against your best interests, as I know you'll see once you calm down.'

Velmond nodded and allowed himself to be persuaded to accompany Bradfield into the refreshment-room for a glass of wine, while Lucy remained with Lady Quainton.

The incident had been observed only by those in the immediate vicinity, and by the time Velmond returned to the drawing-room all seemed as before except for the absence of Mr Yarnton.

Velmond no longer wished to remain at the soirée, however. Having ascertained that Lucy was of the same mind, he went to retrieve his outdoor things from the gentlemen's cloakroom. She lingered for a parting word with Lady Quainton.

She was about to move away when her husband came rushing back into the room, a distraught look on his face which caused those standing near the exit to break off their talk and stare at him.

'Wetherby – for God's sake where's Wetherby?' he cried in urgent tones. 'Ah, there you are!'

He pounced upon the doctor, who was among those near the door by which he had just entered, and seized his arm.

'Quickly – no time to lose! Yarnton – in the cloakroom, some kind of seizure, I think – for God's sake, hurry, man!'

The doctor needed no second bidding but hastened away at once, waving back imperiously those who would have followed him. Only Velmond was permitted to accompany him the few

17

steps along the passage to the small ante-room which had been placed at the disposal of the gentlemen guests.

Word of some crisis quickly circulated among the company and they all gathered round the door of the drawing-room, talking in low tones. Lady Windlesham was leaning on Lady Quainton's arm, looking extremely distressed.

Presently the doctor came slowly back into the room, his face grave. At his heels was Velmond, even more shaken than before.

'What is it?' cried Lady Windlesham, in an unnaturally high, cracked voice. 'Mr Yarnton – pray tell us – how is he?'

Dr Wetherby signalled to a curious, hovering footman to bring forward a chair for his mistress. She sank into it thankfully, her eyes fixed painfully on the doctor's face.

'I regret to inform you, ma'am,' he said quietly, 'that Mr Yarnton is dead. There is nothing I can do for him.'

A gasp of horror ran round the guests.

'Some kind of seizure, was it?' asked one of the men. 'Velmond said – '

Dr Wetherby cut him short. 'No. I fear the situation's more serious than that. You must all prepare yourselves for a shock; the ladies had best be seated.'

He waited some minutes while this instruction was obeyed.

'Mr Yarnton's death was not due to sudden illness,' he resumed. 'I found him strangled with his own cravat – pressure on the carotid artery. Impossible to be self-inflicted. This is murder, Lady Windlesham. It is our painful duty to inform Bow Street.'

Chapter II

Law enforcement in London had for more than sixty years been centred on a building in Bow Street. It was the house where the novelist Henry Fielding had lived after being appointed chief magistrate for Westminster in 1749. Here he revolutionized the ineffectual policing of the metropolis by setting up a small force of specialist thief-takers, or Runners as they soon came to be called, and persuading the Government to pay a modest annual fee to the men for their services.

After his death his half-brother Sir John Fielding, the Blind Beak, expanded the service. He founded a highway foot patrol and set up a criminal record office, eventually producing a gazette which circulated particulars of wanted criminals.

So successful was the Bow Street system in combating crime that in 1792 the Government reluctantly passed a Bill appointing seven other similar police offices in the metropolis. This move was followed later by the founding of the River Police and later still by a mounted patrol covering the roads out of London after dark. The Bow Street office still retained its former importance, however, and by an unwritten law only Bow Street Runners were allowed to be sent into the country to pursue investigations.

Sir Nathaniel Conant, chief magistrate at Bow Street, was not at all happy. It was not that he was unaccustomed to dealing with cases of murder. In the tough areas near the river where drunken sailors, lightermen and prostitutes abounded, violent quarrels frequently arose which ended in a knifing. The same was true of the rookeries of crime which lay close to the City and even around Westminster Abbey; robbery with violence was rife and sometimes the violence ended in murder.

But murder, in Sir Nathaniel's view, was a crime of the lower orders. There had been occasions in the past, of course, before duelling fell out of favour, when a gentleman would fatally wound his opponent and be obliged either to flee the country or else stand trial for murder. That was quite another matter from the strangling of a guest at a *ton* party in the West End of London.

And it really did look as if the deed must have been done by a member of the Quality.

Two of his most reliable Runners had been assisting him on the case. They had quickly established that there was no way in which an intruder could have gained access to the house unseen and that it must therefore be an inside crime. There was no evidence of robbery as the dead man was still in possession of his money and valuables. They had questioned the servants rigorously but failed to find anything suspicious in their depositions. Moreover all of them had been in Lady Windlesham's employment for several years and had respectable backgrounds.

Reluctantly Sir Nathaniel decided that the guests must be questioned.

This he undertook personally, aided by one of his assistant magistrates, both proceeding with the utmost tact and delicacy. It was not a pleasant business. The Quality were not accustomed to be required to give an account of their actions and most of them resented it deeply. Several announced their intention of registering a complaint with the Home Secretary.

When asked about their relations with the dead man one and all shrugged off the question. They doubted if he had possessed any close friends; certainly no one present admitted to being on such terms with him. He was variously described as amusing, a wag, a bit of a scandalmonger and 'not quite the thing'. Lady Windlesham freely acknowledged that he was asked to parties for his entertainment value and not because he was a popular figure.

'Would you say he had enemies, sir?' Conant asked deferentially of Cleveland. 'Someone present who bore him a grudge?'

'Too strong a word, enemies,' objected the politician. 'His

quips occasionally stung but I don't think anyone took him seriously. Certainly not seriously enough to do away with him.'

Nevertheless, by means of a hint dropped here and an incautious word there, Conant came to learn of the quarrel between Yarnton and Velmond.

This altered matters. Not only had Lord Velmond attempted to assault the victim but he had been the one to discover the body. Questioned, he admitted that there had been no one else in the cloakroom at the time; so there were no witnesses to his assertion that when he came upon Yarnton the man was already dead.

Conant and his fellow magistrate looked grave.

Having established that not much more than half an hour could have elapsed between Velmond's quarrel with Yarnton and the former's visit to the cloakroom, it was not difficult to fix an approximate time for the murder. It then became important to know if any other gentleman had visited the cloakroom during this period and had seen the victim alive. No one admitted to doing so; and it was impossible to check because the attendant had been missing from his post – a dereliction of duty for which Lady Windlesham's butler indicated that heads would roll.

'Don't help us at all,' said Conant's assistant in an undertone to his superior. 'Looks as if this Lord Velmond's our man.'

'Tut, tut, a peer of the realm,' objected Sir Nathaniel.

'There was that Lord Cochrane involved in the Stock Exchange fraud two years ago,' the other reminded him.

'Quite a different affair, my dear fellow; stocks and shares are a natural medium, one might say, for – um – any inclination towards crime which might be harboured by the Quality. But murder is a vastly different kettle of fish. We must proceed very carefully in this affair – indeed, with the utmost circumspection. More evidence is needed, much more, before we venture upon an arrest. We must look into the deceased's affairs, search his residence for any clue to a more convincing motive than a few hasty words exchanged between two gentlemen at a party.'

This was agreed; but nevertheless Velmond was requested, in the most diffident way possible, not to leave London until further investigations had been pursued. Although this was not mentioned to Velmond, Runner Joseph Watts, formerly a sergeant in Wellington's army and a man of resource and initiative, was instructed to keep strict surveillance on the young nobleman.

Nothing was said between the Velmonds on the subject which was occupying the minds of both. On the following day they went about their own concerns, scarcely meeting until late in the afternoon when Velmond strode into the library and found his wife sitting there.

She gave a start and dropped the book which had rested in her hands open at the same page for the past half hour.

He stooped automatically to retrieve it.

'Thank you,' she said in a small voice, taking it from him.

'This damnable business!' he exclaimed bitterly. 'There's been a man following me about all day! He may think I don't notice but I ain't such a gudgeon as that. A Runner, I collect. Next thing they'll haul me off to Newgate, I suppose. Oh, well – damned if I care more than half.'

'Oh, you mustn't say so!' she replied in tones of deep distress. 'They cannot possibly think that you – that you'd do such a thing,' she finished weakly.

'Why not?' He fixed her with a searching look. 'I was furious with the man, wasn't I? Do *you* believe I couldn't have done it? Answer me truthfully!'

Tears brimmed over her eyes and fell on to the book on her lap. He snatched it away angrily, flinging it upon a side table.

'I see you prefer not to answer. My own wife! What chance that anyone else could believe me innocent?'

She started up, attempting to embrace him, but he pushed her away.

'But I do, I do!' she protested, sobbing. 'Oh, if only it had never happened! If only – '

'If only that scoundrel hadn't seen you on your clandestine outing,' he finished in a biting tone. 'Where *were* you going, I wonder? Useless to ask – a husband is always the last to know in these matters.'

She made a strong effort to pull herself together. She had

been expecting this question and had her answer ready.

'I would have told you, but that I thought you might disapprove of my trying to help. It was for Sally, you know – '

'Sally? Who in thunder's Sally?'

'She's one of the housemaids; she does the fire in my room. Her family were in trouble – they're terribly poor, you know – and I wanted to assist them. And so – and so – ' She hesitated, then went on in a rush, 'I didn't like to take your carriage into such a low quarter so I took a hackney, and I wore a veil so that if by chance anyone saw me – '

She could not continue under his penetrating stare. Would he believe her? She had done her best, and it was not so very far from the truth. Sally would bear her out, if questioned. But oh, dear God, if only it had not been necessary to deceive him!

'And you expect me to believe this farrago?' he demanded contemptuously. 'Don't concern yourself, I've no intention of questioning the housemaid! I wonder, though – ' As a sudden thought struck him he continued, – 'Where *Mr Thompson* comes into this story? I noticed you changed colour when that fellow Yarnton mentioned his name.'

Again her cheeks paled and she looked as if she might swoon. He pushed her back into a chair, although not roughly. He rang for a servant and one of the footmen appeared.

'My lady is unwell. Bring her maid,' he ordered as he strode from the room.

He neither knew nor cared where he was going as he rushed out of the house and through the busy streets. He was halted at last by someone calling his name. He turned, like a man in a dream.

'Where the deuce are you galloping off to, George, old fellow?'

The speaker was a man of his own age, a little above medium height with a spare yet muscular frame. His hat was perched carelessly on a mop of curling dark hair that partly concealed a high forehead, and his brown eyes glinted with alert intelligence. He put out a hand to grasp Velmond's, grinning at him.

'You appear to be propelled by one of Boulton and Watt's steam engines, George. Whither away?'

Velmond wrung the proffered hand cordially, his face

clearing a little.

'Good to see you, Justin. So you're back.'

The other shook his head quizzically. 'No, am I?'

'Don't be a gudgeon. Where have you been *this* time?'

'France. Took a notion to see the standing stones at Carnac. Ever been there?'

Velmond shook his head.

'Should do. Most impressive. Beats our own Avebury circle into a cocked hat. Though mind you, Stonehenge – '

He broke off, studying his friend's face with a shrewd yet sympathetic expression.

'Don't think you're quite in the mood for talk of prehistoric sites. Something's up, George – care to tell me about it?'

'Yes, b'God, I would,' replied Velmond fervently. 'But not here, I think.' He glanced round the crowded pavement, aware for the first time of his surroundings. 'And I don't particularly wish to return home just at present,' he added slowly.

'So that leaves either one of the clubs, where it's difficult to be private, or my place,' said the Honourable Justin Rutherford with an air of decision. 'The latter, do you agree?'

Velmond nodded and they fell into step side by side until they had covered the short distance to Albemarle Street, where Rutherford had a set of rooms.

Only commonplaces passed between them until they were comfortably seated, one either side of a glowing fire with a decanter of wine and glasses at hand.

Justin raised his glass. 'And now a long overdue toast to you and your bride, my dear chap. I hear she's the most stunning creature – lucky dog!'

'Thanks. Yes, Lucy *is* lovely.'

'Do I detect a hint of reticence? Come now, I'm quite prepared to endure your raptures – least an old friend can do, what? Rhapsodize on, George, and damn'd be him who first cries "Hold, enough", to quote the Bard.' He broke off and set down his glass, his eyes alert. 'You're not in the mood for funning, either. Best tell me what the trouble is. Two heads better than one, y'know.'

Velmond told him, while the other listened attentively. In spite of a sometimes frivolous exterior Justin Rutherford

24

possessed a powerful intellect which was at once engaged by the mystery attending Yarnton's death.

'Well, it wasn't you, so who was it?' he asked at the conclusion of Velmond's account. 'Any theories?'

'You accept that I'm not guilty, then?' Velmond countered, a slight tremor in his voice. 'You take my word for it?'

'Indubitably. Not your style, is it? You might land a man a facer in such circumstances, might even call him out,' said Justin judicially. 'Murder – no. Not you.'

Velmond seemed much moved by this and murmured his gratitude.

'Stuff! One doesn't know a man all those years at Oxford, and since, without learning something about him. But have you no suspicions about any of the others present? Anything you noticed?'

'Can't say I did. He wasn't liked, of course, but can't think anyone would consider him worth swinging for. Besides, I was too annoyed at the time to trouble myself about other people's reactions.'

'Hm. This innuendo concerning Lady Velmond which aroused your ire,' said Justin carefully. 'I imagine she's explained about that?'

'Oh, yes,' replied Velmond with a bitter edge to his tone. 'She's explained, for sure. Only – '

He broke off and tossed down the wine in his glass.

'Look here, Justin – as you say, we've been friends a long time – devilish good friends. I know I can trust you. The thing is, I can't believe the story Lucy told me. See what you think.'

He repeated Lucy's tale.

'Of course,' he concluded, 'she *might* have done something like that. She's generous, compassionate and impulsive enough. But why the devil couldn't she simply have given the girl some money to take home herself? No need that I can see for Lucy personally to go to all that trouble in the business. Besides, it's not only that the story's too thin. There's this other matter of a man named Thompson whom Yarnton quizzed us all about – she knew that name, I'll swear. She turned as pale as a ghost when she heard it, though I didn't realize that was the reason until afterwards, when I taxed her with it again this afternoon. Same reaction – devilish near swooned.'

'And how do you account for her lying to you? That's to say, if she really *is* lying.'

'I think,' said Velmond explosively, 'that she had an assignation with this fellow Thompson, whoever he may be, and that Yarnton knew of it by some means. Trust him to sniff out that kind of thing!'

'My dear old George,' said Justin in a voice of deep concern. 'Why on earth should you entertain such an outrageous notion? Not long married, and Lady Velmond so young and innocent–'

Velmond repeated the last words scornfully. 'Young, yes, but how do I know she's as innocent as she seems? I tell you, Justin, her father and brother are deep in the river Tick and promoted our marriage as their only lifeline! As for Lucy, I *thought* she loved me as I do her, but how do I know that? She's reserved with me – I supposed that might be the shyness of a young bride and it would wear off in time. But perhaps it's because she considers ours a marriage of convenience and all the time she's given her heart elsewhere, to this man Thompson! But I tell you, I'll find that scoundrel if it's the last thing I do, and when I do find him, I'll, I'll – '

'Commit murder?' asked Justin quietly. 'No, George, I don't think you will. Instead, perhaps you'll permit me first to look into this matter of *Yarnton*'s murder and see what emerges. You know, old fellow, people – especially females – often make a mystery of some damn silly thing which isn't of the least consequence to anyone else and only exists in their imagination. So I beg you, don't do anything hasty until I've had the opportunity to pursue a few investigations myself into Yarnton's unfortunate demise. The affair intrigues me. You say my godmother, Cassandra Quainton, was one of the guests? I'll have a word with her – she's an unusually observant female.'

'I must say it's a profound relief to know that someone doesn't think I'm a murderer,' remarked Velmond in a slightly more cheerful tone. 'And I know from past experience that you're a bit of a wizard at solving puzzles, so perhaps you'll turn something up. I wonder if that damned Runner has followed me here?' he added in a changed tone, going over to the window and peering out. 'Yes, there the devilish fellow is,

26

leaning against a lamp-post. It's the outside of enough!'

Justin followed him over to the window and glanced outside. Then his gaze sharpened as it lighted upon a stocky individual with a familiar profile of jutting jaw and long, sharp nose.

'Good God, it's Sergeant Watts!' he exclaimed. 'You say he's a Runner, George? He's the man who worked with me during my brief spell in the Peninsular army. I ask you, my dear fellow, what could be more fortunate! I'll fetch him in at once.'

Velmond gave a snort.

'If you've a back way out, I'll be off, then. I've seen enough of him for today. No doubt you'll explain that I'm not fleeing the country!'

Chapter III

'The trouble is, captain,' said Joe Watts, when the two of them were alone together, 'we've precious little to go on in this case. A nice straightforward robbery with violence, now, and we knows where we be. But our first interrogations cleared the domestics, which leaves only the Quality, and *that* Sir Nathaniel don't like at all. Out of his depth, he is. It's my belief as he'd be downright glad to have you take a hand, captain.'

'Forget the "captain", Joe. We're not in the army now. Well, what if you take me to see Sir Nathaniel Conant?'

'Yessir. The only thing is, I'm supposed to be keeping an eye on the gentleman who's just left. Beggin' your pardon, for he's a friend of yours?'

'Take my word for it, Joe, he's not your man. Anyway, I'll make that right with the magistrate.'

Justin's subsequent interview with Conant was extremely affable and ended just as he wished. He was allowed to retain the exclusive services of Runner Watts at the usual fee of one guinea per day and expenses. Conant did not think it necessary to say so, but he intended to put another man on surveillance of Lord Velmond, although he now felt even less certain of the nobleman's guilt. Moreover, Justin was promised access to any further information obtained by the authorities. Some was already to hand.

'We've made inquiries into the deceased's circumstances,' said Conant. 'It transpires that he had little of value to leave and no direct heirs, so that rules out financial gain as a motive for the crime. In a case such as this, a really strong motive would be a clincher, when one considers that almost anyone present could have had the opportunity for the deed. So far, unfortunately, we've failed to uncover a specific motive. It

28

could well be that he was killed for revenge on account of his malicious remarks, but I'm bound to say those who knew him pooh-pooh this notion. All the same, we can't entirely discount it, of course.' He coughed, thinking of the quarrel with Velmond. 'Another motive that frequently occurs in such cases is jealousy. I don't need to point out to you, my dear sir, the strength of feeling when a lady's involved. It's not unknown for a man to kill under its influence. But so far our investigations have failed to discover any emotional entanglement in the deceased's life – indeed, he appears to have been a man without close friends of either sex.'

Justin nodded. 'I collect that not much above half an hour elapsed between Yarnton's quitting the drawing-room and the discovery of his body in the cloakroom? Is there any evidence to show that he went into the cloakroom at once and remained there all the time?'

'Unfortunately, no, sir. He was observed by some of those near the exit to leave the room hurriedly, but there are no witnesses to his movements after that. As there was no servant on duty in the cloakroom at the time, this is scarcely surprising. One would hardly expect the guests to notice.'

'Quite so. One other point occurs to me. It's possible that the murderer may have been still concealed somewhere in the cloakroom when Lord Velmond first entered it, and afterwards, when he came back with the doctor. By the time your people arrived on the scene the fellow could easily have managed to escape, of course. But did your questioning elicit from either of the two gentlemen that they had heard any noise, or sensed anything that would suggest the presence in the room of a third party?'

Sir Nathaniel looked uncomfortable. 'I must admit, Mr Rutherford, that the question was not put to them, but I feel sure they would have mentioned it, had such been the case.'

Justin nodded. 'Thank you, Sir Nathaniel. You have been very good and I'm much obliged. I wonder if I could trouble you a little further, and request a list of all the guests present at the soirée?'

Conant willingly complied and Justin Rutherford took his leave.

'Well, what would you like me to do now, sir?' asked Watts as they left the Bow Street office.

'Do you know the area around Petticoat Lane, Joe?'

'Lor' luv ye, sir, like my own backyard! Not a place to venture after dark, though, unless you're in company,' he added.

'Leave it until tomorrow, then. What I'd like you to do is see if you can find someone in that vicinity who observed a young and pretty lady, veiled, alighting there from a hackney one day during the past week or so. I wish to discover where she went, if possible. You'll know the kind of thing.'

'Right, sir. Mayn't get the information for a day or so, though. Report back to your place, sir?'

Justin nodded. 'I'll give orders for you to be admitted at any time, and if I'm not here write me a note and leave it on my desk yonder.'

He indicated a mahogany writing desk against one wall with a number of neatly disposed files on its surface.

'And you'd better leave me a direction where I may get in touch with you if needed,' he added.

When Watts had gone Justin sat down at his desk and drew the long guest list from his pocket.

He studied it with a frown. The usual people had attended Lady Windlesham's soirée, allowing for the fact that it had been held in mid-March, before the season had really begun. Most of the guests were known to him in a casual way, though few more intimately. He would need assistance to sort them out.

He glanced at the clock. Scarcely the right time for a social call, but he knew he could depend upon a welcome in that quarter at any hour of the day.

He was fortunate enough to find his godmother, Lady Quainton, at home and for once alone. She was delighted to see him, insisting that he should stay to dine with her.

'That's to say, unless you've anything of more interest to do,' she added laughing, 'for I'm certain there must be scores of females in Town positively languishing for your presence!'

30

He smiled quizzically. 'So I always hope, ma'am, but I fear they have a disconcerting habit of getting themselves wed to another in my absence.'

'That is quite your own fault, my dear Justin. You should remain here long enough to marry one of them yourself. Do you not feel that perhaps it is time you settled down?'

She kept her tone light, but in fact the question was one which she often considered in all seriousness.

He grimaced. 'Settled down! It has an ominous ring, ma'am, a suggestion of stagnation which I fear doesn't appeal. Fortunately, as a younger son I have no responsibilities of title or estate. Frankly, I rejoice in my freedom.' His tone changed. 'But tell me of the exciting events which have occurred in Town recently. I saw George Velmond today and hear that the poor devil is pretty well suspected of murder.'

Her face became grave. 'Yes, I believe there is some suspicion hanging over him. Quite absurd, of course, to anyone who knows him as we do, but circumstances were unfortunate, one must confess. I dare say he told you all about it?'

He nodded. 'But as I understand you were present, I've come to you to fill in the gaps, for you're quite the most observant person of my acquaintance.'

She gave a whimsical pout. 'Fie, for shame, and I thought you'd sought me out for the sake of my own delightful company! But there, when a female is stricken in years – '

He laughed and patted her hand. 'So stricken, godmama, that she puts every other female of her years to the blush! Not a single grey hair among the rich brown, and a complexion any young girl might envy! I tell you, I live in daily expectation that you'll announce your second marriage.'

'Pooh, what a shameless flatterer you are, boy,' she answered severely, though she looked pleased. 'You have no need to try and turn me up sweet! As for second marriages, I don't wish to brag, but there have been opportunities.' Her tone sobered. 'But you see, Harry Quainton, God rest him, is a difficult man to replace. I'm well enough suited as I am.'

He nodded and they were silent for a moment.

'You may as well know, ma'am, that my interest in this affair has been aroused to the pitch where I mean to discover who *did* commit the murder. In fact, I've seen the Bow Street magistrate and hired one of his Runners, a fellow I worked with in the army, to assist me in my inquiries.'

'Indeed? Well, I'm not so surprised as I might be, knowing your liking for solving puzzles and, of course, your long friendship with young Velmond. Ask me anything you wish and I'll endeavour to provide satisfactory answers.'

'First of all, who do you suppose might have perpetrated the deed? Woman's intuition, y'know.'

She shook her head. 'I'm at a loss to suggest anyone. Several people must have disliked the man, but murder! Only a powerful incentive could produce such a dire action.'

'Exactly so. Bow Street investigations have so far failed to produce such an incentive.' He briefly outlined to her what he had learnt. 'Velmond's motive remains the most outstanding, unfortunately. Was there anything else you heard Yarnton say which might have affected another of the guests powerfully, although it didn't actually precipitate a scene such as poor George made? Something, perhaps, which simmered in the mind and later produced murder?'

'Well, yes, there was,' she said quickly. 'Only a short while before Velmond overheard that unfortunate remark, Yarnton made a cryptic reference to some unknown man before a small group of us. It was to a Mr Thompson.'

Justin's eyes lit up. 'Ah! Yes, George told me of that – said that his wife turned pale at the name. He seemed to believe – this I know will go no further, ma'am – that Lady Velmond's mysterious visit to Petticoat Lane was to keep an assignation with this Thompson, whoever he may be.'

'Oh, dear, oh dear!' Lady Quainton was distressed but she rallied almost at once. 'But that's absurd – it must be! Whoever keeps assignations in such a locality? Besides, I'll not believe that Lucilla Velmond doesn't positively dote on her husband; you should only see the girl look at him when he isn't noticing! Another thing, and more to the point, Justin, is that she wasn't the only one to be affected by mention of that name, unless I'm much mistaken.'

'Which I dare swear you are not. Tell me precisely what occurred: who was in the group, how Yarnton phrased his remark, every detail you can recall,' he demanded quickly.

'Let me think. There were eight of us together at that time – myself and Lady Kinver, the Velmonds, Mr and Mrs Cleveland, Mr Bradfield and Dr Wetherby. You're a little acquainted with them all, I believe?'

He nodded, not wishing to interrupt. Her face wore an abstracted look as she attempted to recall the scene in precise detail.

'Yarnton insinuated himself among us, in that odious way of his, and made some feline remark to Sophia Cleveland – she dyes her hair but thinks no one knows it! Then he turned his attention to the men and quizzed Cleveland about engaging in business discussions at a soirée, because Cleveland had just been conferring with his secretary, Peyton. Oh, I forgot, Peyton was there too, though he'd come only to bring a message to his employer. Anyway,' she resumed, 'Yarnton went on to say that life was full of mysteries and that one in particular had been puzzling him of late. Then he asked if anyone could tell him who Mr Thompson was – though he said it as if he knew all the time.'

'No one obliged, I collect. But you did observe reactions in someone other than Lady Velmond?'

'I could scarce avoid noticing Jane Kinver give a nervous start, for she was close beside me. But she *is* a very high-strung woman, you know, and that might have meant nothing,' she said doubtfully. 'I'm almost certain, too, that I saw a slight spasm pass over Cleveland's face – gone in a moment, for those political gentlemen aren't the kind to betray their feelings. Nevertheless, the impression remains with me that the name had some significance for him. As for the other gentlemen present, Velmond and Dr Wetherby at once demanded to be told what he meant. But he refused to enlighten them, beyond indicating that they could help him if they chose, as the man Thompson was present, and not so very far away – or words to that effect.'

Justin's glance sharpened. 'Could you possibly contrive, dearest godmama, to recall the *exact* words? I have the persuasion that they may be important.'

She puzzled over this request for a few moments but

33

eventually managed to do as he asked.

'Ah!' he exclaimed. 'And what impression did his words make upon you, may I ask?'

'A vastly uncomfortable one, I declare, for he made it sound as if this person Thompson were among our own group, which would be complete nonsense! But that is the way in which Yarnton goes – I should say used to go – to work. His aim was ever to make people uncomfortable – what a dreadful epitaph for a man!'

'Indeed it is. You didn't mention the reactions of Velmond's friend, Bradfield, and the secretary to Cleveland. Perhaps you hadn't time to notice?'

She creased her brows again in an effort of recollection.

'I believe young Peyton frowned,' she said at last, 'though whether in puzzlement or disapproval, I couldn't say. As for Mr Bradfield, come to think of it, he appeared slightly amused. But then, most people were amused by Yarnton.'

'Hm.' It was Justin's turn to consider what had been reported to him. 'So three people at least seem to have betrayed some reaction to the mention of this mysterious Thompson,' he said. 'Could there be any connection between those three beyond the bounds of mere acquaintance, do you know? For instance, is Lucilla Velmond on friendly terms with either the Clevelands or with Lady Kinver, or both?'

'Oh, no, I'm certain of that. She met them for the first time at that soirée. Indeed, she was telling me how little acquaintance she possesses as yet in London. The only person she spoke of knowing at all was your niece, Anthea.'

'Anthea! Ha, better and better!' exclaimed Justin. 'I think we shall go on a deal more quickly once we clear this little mystery of Lady Velmond's out of the way, and Anthea's the very girl to tackle that.'

'What is your interest in Lady Velmond?' asked Anthea Rutherford with a quizzical glance of her extremely fine dark eyes. 'Do you wish me to help you seduce her?'

He regarded her severely. 'If your mama had any notion of the low moral tone of your discourse, she would pack you off to

34

the country with a strict chaperone,' he warned her.

'Oh, fustian! I think she would merely say that I'm distressingly like you – something which I'm quite accustomed to hearing whenever my conduct deviates from what is considered proper.'

'Let us trust you'll grow out of it, my dear niece. For your information, however, let me state that I'm perfectly capable of conducting my seductions unaided.'

She smiled, dimpling her cheeks. 'Oh, that I do believe, my dear uncle.'

He grinned. 'Well, since we've done with the formalities, let's be serious for a moment. No one from our family was present at Lady Windlesham's soirée, but I don't doubt that gossip has supplied all the details of what occurred there. Not to make a long story of it, my friend Velmond is under suspicion for Yarnton's murder and I mean to clear him.'

'You do?' She clasped her hands together in excitement. 'Oh, what fun! How perfectly splendid, Justin!'

All attempts by Anthea's parents to insist on a more proper form of address for her relative had met with failure. Meeting with no support from the principal in the affair, they had finally abandoned the unequal struggle. They stipulated only that she should show more circumspection outside the family circle.

'I don't know about fun, but I must admit to being intrigued by the business, quite apart from wishing to help old George. I know one should never confide in females, but I think – only *think*, mark you – that you may be an exception, Anthea.'

'Oh, yes,' she breathed, leaning forward with a glint in her eyes which made her resemble Justin strongly, 'yes, indeed you may. I won't breathe a word! See this wet, see this dry!'

She drew a finger across her slender neck in the time-honoured childish gesture.

'Well, just make sure you don't,' he retorted darkly. 'The point is this. George's wife has some secret – probably the silliest thing, but important to her – which is clouding the issue. I'll explain, if you don't interrupt.'

She listened avidly while he repeated what he had learned so far of events on the night of the murder. Her eyes opened wide but she obediently kept quiet until he had finished.

'The girl's very taken with you, so Lady Quinton assures me,' he concluded. 'Could you pursue the acquaintance and possibly persuade her to confide this secret to you? I feel convinced that it's not at all what Velmond suspects, so you need not fear that the knowledge will place you in an invidious position. And possibly it may help to clear her husband of suspicion and point the way to the real murderer.'

'I very much wish to become friendly with Lady Velmond on my own account,' replied Anthea nodding. 'She is not at all like me, you know, which promises well for friendship, as two likes seldom deal well together! Besides, she is a blonde and I'm a brunette, so we shan't be in competition, shall we?'

Chapter IV

No one knew better than Joseph Watts that London was an incongruous amalgam of the magnificent and the squalid. Behind the fine squares and wide, stately thoroughfares with their elegant residences and glittering shops lay a dingier, noisome area of narrow, ill-lit and filthy alleys with dilapidated tenements where dubious characters eked out a precarious existence as pickpockets or by other forms of crime. Even the Runners did not care to enter these rookeries singly after nightfall, so it was broad daylight when he turned out of Houndsditch into Petticoat Lane.

At his appearance a surprising number of sleazy individuals found urgent business elsewhere. Although the Runners wore no distinguishing uniform, the denizens of this neighbourhood found no difficulty in recognizing them for what they were.

One wizened old woman with a barrow of vegetables stood her ground, however, ostensibly plying a legitimate trade.

Watts knew her well, for she could be found most days somewhere in this area. He nodded.

'How do, Poll. Still at it, I see?'

She glared defiantly back at him. 'Whad yer mean? 'Course I'm sellin' me veg, same as always. No law agin that, is there?'

'Oh, no, as long as that's all y'r doing. I just wonder if it is, now?'

He picked up one of the languid, yellowing cabbages from the barrow, surveying it disparagingly. She snatched it hastily away from him.

''Ere now, none o' that,' she snarled. 'Don't go a-spoilin' o' me goods!'

'Spoilin' that lot – that's rich, that is. But then it don't much matter what's atop, as long as there's something worthwhile underneath, do it, ma?'

'Whad yer mean?' Her tone was aggressive but there was a trace of uneasiness beneath it.

'Ye knows well enough. Fine hiding place for pickings from them young rascals hereabouts. Don't fret, though' – as she began to protest – 'I'm not after you for that today. It'll keep. No, what I want is a bit of information.'

She cast a worried glance about her, but there was no one within earshot, although she knew only too well that several pairs of eyes would be observing everything from safe concealment.

'I 'bain't no nark!' she protested in a voice she hoped would carry to some of the hidden observers.

'Nothing o' that kind,' he reassured her. 'What I wants to know is, did you see a gentry mort, young, wearin' a veil, getting out o' a hackney hereabouts? Could be a week ago, more or less.'

'Dunno,' she hedged, eyeing him warily. 'Can't be expected to see everythink, now, can I?'

'Not much misses you, I'll be bound. And there can't be so many ladies visiting these parts, nor many hackneys, neither. Come on, Poll, rattle that head o' yourn, or what passes for such.'

'What's it to ye?' She looked cunningly at him. 'What's it worth, mister?'

'D'ye reckon ye can bargain with me? Why, for two pins I'd search that barrow o' yourn – '

'No call to be 'asty,' she said quickly, shrinking back. 'Ay, I calls it to mind now, right enough. There was a 'ackney come round the corner 'ere, an' this flash moll gets out. Fair scuttles back into the 'Oundsditch, she do, wiv one o' they prigs a-follerin' 'er, but 'e didn't get nuffink, 'cos she was too quick into the shop.'

'What shop?'

She sniffed. 'Why, Beaver's, of course, bad cess to 'im. No use to the likes o' us, 'e 'bain't.'

Watts nodded. He knew Beaver, a pawnbroker in a respectable though modest line of business who so far had never been suspected of receiving stolen goods, unlike most in that district.

'Too honest for you lot,' he agreed. 'Did you see the lady

38

return?'

She shook her head. 'No, 'cos the 'ack turned round a bit further down an' picked 'er up outside Beaver's.'

'How d' you know that, I wonder?'

She shrugged. 'The lad told me; 'e follered 'er, but t'weren't no use.'

'You mean the prig – pickpocket? Didn't get anything for his pains, eh? Well, I don't doubt ye'll benefit from his pickings most times. Oh, don't trouble yourself to deny it, woman. I knows your lay and one o' these days I'll do ye for it, mark my words.'

'That's gratitood, that is,' she sniffed as he walked away.

He turned the corner into Houndsditch and entered the pawnbroker's premises.

Anthea Rutherford lost no time in following up Justin's suggestion, calling upon Lucilla Velmond that very same day. She took only her maid with her so that there might be more possibility of a tête-à-tête than if Lady Rutherford had accompanied her.

She was fortunate in finding that Velmond was out and Lucy quite alone. She was warmly received and soon the two were enjoying a quiet little feminine chat together on fashions and other such innocuous subjects. It was obvious that Lucy welcomed the other girl's friendly overtures; but nevertheless there was an air of constraint about her.

'We must see more of each other, my dear Lady Velmond,' said Anthea when she rose to go after having outstayed the normal time for a social call. 'Are you engaged tomorrow morning? Would you care to drive out in the park with me, if it should prove fine?'

'Oh, yes, I should like that of all things,' said Lucy enthusiastically. 'As to engagements, I have few at present, since so far I've not had time to form any acquaintance. And I believe my husband' – her voice dropped and her face clouded – 'is too occupied just now to be at home a great deal.'

'Then I'll call for you at eleven o'clock, if that's convenient?' asked Anthea, extending her hand in parting. This was agreed.

39

The outing was the start of daily meetings, and before a week had elapsed the two were on easy enough terms to be calling each other by first names. Anthea encouraged her new friend to talk about her past life in Somerset, but she learned nothing which could throw any light on Lucy's mysterious visit to Petticoat Lane.

She was bemoaning this fact to Justin when they met after an interval of several days.

'Well, as to that,' he said consolingly, 'I've received some information from Watts, the Runner. I now know where Lady Velmond was going when Yarnton saw her. But,' – he frowned – 'the reason for her visit remains obscure.'

'Tell me at once,' she urged, an eager expression on her face.

'She visited a pawnbroker's in Houndsditch in order to raise money on a piece of jewellery – an old-fashioned necklace, such as I dare say a young female wouldn't wish to wear, but which was valuable, nevertheless.'

She gasped. 'Good heavens, Justin! A pawnbroker's! Why in the world should she need to raise money? Surely Velmond is wealthy enough to supply all her wants?'

'There may be times, chit, when a female don't wish her husband to know what she's spending.'

'You think she's unduly extravagant?' she asked doubtfully. 'And yet, when we went shopping together yesterday she didn't impress me as being an impulsive buyer. Quite the reverse, in fact, for although she doted on a bonnet we saw, she said only that she would think about it. She didn't purchase a single item, whereas I – '

He laughed. 'Don't tell me! The carriage was so loaded with bandboxes, that you were both obliged to walk home. And now you've outrun the constable, and want a loan – how much?'

He drew out his pocketbook, grinning at her.

'You're a beast! But seriously, Justin, I can't believe that's the reason Lucy needs the money. Can she have been gaming?' she asked doubtfully. 'But then, she scarce knows anyone in Town with whom to play.'

'That notion had entered my brilliant mind, too, so I asked George if his wife was fond of cards and so on. He said he doubted her ability to distinguish one suit from another.'

40

'It has me in a puzzle altogether,' admitted Anthea frowning. 'Another notion occurred to me, though, and I think a more likely one. The lady has a brother whose pockets are permanently to let, by all I hear. It happens that this brother was staying with the Velmonds at about the relevant time. Now, if—'

'Of course!' interrupted Anthea eagerly. 'That is just what Lucy would do, judging by what I already know of her! She wouldn't like to ask her husband for money and I dare say her brother wouldn't either, so she hit upon this way of assisting him. But he must be an odiously selfish man to let her do such a thing, do you not think, Justin?'

'A dashed loose screw, by all accounts,' agreed Justin. 'But I'd like you to obtain confirmation of this, if you possibly can, my dear. And we're still left with the mystery of Thompson. I've been working on that myself for the past few days.'

'Indeed? In what way, may I ask?'

'By haunting the clubs and chatting to those who were present at that fateful soirée. No difficulty in getting them to talk about the murder – it's quite eclipsed Byron's exploits as a subject for conversation. I haven't yet managed to work my way completely through the guest list but what I have discovered so far is helpful.'

'Helpful? Oh, don't be so teasing, Justin! How is it helpful?'

'Well, curiously enough, Yarnton doesn't seem to have posed the question about the mysterious Thompson's identity to any others except the group surrounding Lady Quainton. Significant, I think.'

A few days later Anthea alighted from her carriage outside the Velmonds' house to see Dr Wetherby just leaving the premises. She was acquainted with him as the Rutherfords were among his many fashionable patients.

'Oh dear,' she exclaimed, having exchanged polite greetings. 'There's no one ill in the house, I trust?'

'Nothing serious, Miss Rutherford, I'm glad to say. Lady Velmond has a slight disorder of the nerves, merely, and I've prescribed a sedative for her.'

'I was about to call on her. I suppose that will be suitable, or do you advise against it?' asked Anthea dubiously.

'Not at all,' he replied in a hearty tone. 'A little feminine company will do her ladyship a deal of good. It will prevent her from brooding overmuch on this, ah, unfortunate situation concerning Lord Velmond.'

'Oh, but she needn't concern herself over that,' said Anthea impulsively, 'for my Uncle Justin has the matter in hand and hopes soon to uncover the real murderer!'

'Indeed?' The doctor's bushy eyebrows shot up. 'That would be Mr Justin Rutherford, I presume?'

She nodded.

'One can only trust that your optimism proves well founded, ma'am. I wish you good day.'

He bowed and turned away to where his carriage was waiting.

Anthea ran up the steps and was soon admitted to the morning-room where Lucy was sitting.

'What *is* all this, my dear?' she asked, planting a light kiss on Lucy's pale cheek. 'I collect you're unwell – I just met Dr Wetherby.'

'Oh, it is nothing,' replied Lucy in an attempt at a casual tone. 'I've not been sleeping too well lately, so George would have it that I must see the doctor. But there's no need at all, indeed there is not. Pray do sit down, Anthea, and make yourself comfortable. I am so glad to see you!'

Anthea complied but her keen glance had already noted the pallor of her friend's face and the dark shadows under her eyes. Suddenly she decided to speak out. It was not only curiosity that inspired her now, but a sincere pity. She had grown fond of Lucy.

'Lucy, I know that something has been troubling you for days past and I don't believe it is due altogether to anxiety on your husband's behalf. It's of no use to pretend otherwise, so why do you not confide in me? Surely by now you know me well enough to realize that you may trust me?'

Lucy's lip trembled but she made no answer.

'You need not be concerned about your husband's situation,' Anthea went on reassuringly, 'Justin, my uncle, that is, will find out the real culprit, you may depend, and clear Velmond of

42

all suspicion.'

'Indeed, that's part of my worry.' Lucy's voice shook. 'But you're quite right in thinking there is something besides – so much worse, Anthea! I'm in a frightful fix – I was forced into a monstrous predicament and as a result George thinks – ' She almost broke down but managed to continue after a moment. 'George thinks that I am conducting a liaison with another man! And the worst of all is that I *dare not* confess the truth to him! Oh, what can I do – whatever can I do?'

She broke into distracted sobs.

Anthea moved to sit beside her on the sofa and placed a comforting arm about her.

'There, there, my love. You mustn't try to bear it all yourself – only tell me the *whole* and then we can see what we might do – together.'

Seated before his desk, his brow slightly furrowed in concentration, Justin was busy writing a few notes on the subject of Yarnton's murder. His academic mind moved more smoothly when thoughts were captured on paper. He assembled the known information under headings, then paused, running his fingers through his dark, curly hair.

This certainly disposed of some possible motives for the murder, but one could only theorize about the other possibilities. Why had Yarnton mentioned the name Thompson only to the group with Lady Quainton? What significance could that name have for Lucilla Velmond, assuming that her actions might be accounted for by a loan to her brother? What significance could it have for Lady Kinver and perhaps Cleveland?

Everyone to whom he had spoken was certain that Yarnton never passed an idle remark. There was always a barb in his comments, calculated to prick one or other of those to whom they were addressed. It was possible that Lady Quainton had been mistaken in supposing that those three – Lucilla, Cleveland and Lady Kinver – had reacted to the name. Indeed, she herself had expressed doubts. Nevertheless, from what he knew of her in the past, Justin was inclined to accept her first impressions.

He pushed back his chair and tapped his fingers abstractedly on the paper. More facts were needed, more investigation. He added a memorandum to his list:

Watts   Any clue to Thompson among Yarnton's papers?
Lady Q   Ask her to question Lady K about Thompson.

He paused on this second note. He knew of no one who could question Cleveland casually about the name Thompson, and at present he could not think of an oblique approach. His secretary, perhaps? It was tricky.

A tap on the door recalled him from his cogitations. He threw down his pen impatiently, calling out permission to enter. His manservant appeared.

'Beg pardon for disturbing you, sir, but Miss Rutherford wishes to see you. Most insistent.'

'Oh, very well, Selby. Admit her.'

Anthea came hurriedly into the room as Justin rose from his desk. He smiled and directed her to a chair.

'You've arrived in a good hour, as the French say. I need distraction. Can I offer you some refreshment – tea, coffee, ratafia?'

'No, nothing, thank you,' she answered quickly. 'I'm here on urgent business! Justin, I think you should know – '

He interrupted her with a slight gesture and turned to dismiss Selby, who closed the door quietly behind him.

'Now tell me,' he invited, his keen eyes detecting the anxiety in her face.

'It's Lucy!' declared Anthea in a rush. 'Justin, she's in the most monstrous trouble! She's confided the whole to me and I've persuaded her to accompany me here to see you – she's waiting outside. Oh, Justin, it's far worse than we supposed. She's being blackmailed!'

Chapter V

Good God!'

'Isn't it frightful? I thought you would need to see her yourself, for you'll know just what questions to put to her. But you will be gentle with her, won't you? Because naturally she is in a vastly nervous state, not to mention her embarrassment at being obliged to face you – someone she scarce knows. Only I represented strongly to her the necessity – '

'Thompson?' demanded Justin quickly.

'Yes, how did you guess?'

'Never mind that. Go and fetch your friend in, my dear. Meanwhile I'll get Selby to bring some wine.'

This was done and soon a shrinking Lucy was seated on the edge of one of Justin's easy chairs with Anthea close beside her.

Justin, having greeted his guest formally, poured out a small glass of wine and handed it to her.

'Pray drink that, Lady Velmond. It will put some heart into you.'

Lucy waved it feebly away. 'Oh, no, I don't think – indeed, I don't want anything – '

'I insist,' he said gently. 'Think of it as medicinal.'

She took it, then, in a trembling hand and sipped cautiously at its contents. After a few moments a little colour came back into her face.

'Perhaps,' said Justin in quiet but matter-of-fact tones, 'you would like to tell me about your predicament?'

She looked at him uncertainly, her cheeks flushing.

Anthea leaned over to take the wine glass from her.

'Pray don't be nervous, Lucy,' she urged in an encouraging tone. 'You do not know Justin, Mr Rutherford, at all well, but he has been a close friend of your husband for years, and I assure you he may be trusted implicitly.'

'But – but I don't wish my husband to learn of this,' stammered Lucy. 'Everything I've done – and – and suffered, has been to prevent him from knowing.'

'If anyone is to tell him, it will be you, ma'am, and not myself, I assure you,' said Justin quietly. 'But,' – as he saw her open her mouth to utter a protest – 'that decision is for you to make. And now, if you could explain to me precisely what happened, it would assist matters considerably. Shall we start with the demand for blackmail?'

His calm, impersonal manner had its effect. She leaned back more easily in her chair and managed to speak coherently.

'It was a letter. It came about three weeks since and it said that unless I wished my husband to be informed about – ' she gulped, then went on steadily, 'certain events from my past, when I was a schoolgirl, I was to send five hundred pounds to the person named in the letter.'

'A Mr Thompson, I think?'

She nodded, a look of surprise on her face. 'Yes, how did you know? Oh, but I suppose Anthea must have told you before I came into the room.'

'No, my niece told me none of the details. I preferred to hear them from you. But the name Thompson appeared to distress you when it was spoken by the murdered man at Lady Windlesham's soirée. No matter – tell me, ma'am, do you still have this letter?'

She shuddered. 'Oh, no, I burnt it. It was horrible! I could not bear to keep it by me – besides, it wasn't safe.'

'A pity, but your reasons are understandable. Was it handwritten? Did it come through the post?'

'No, it was made up of printed words cut from some journal or other, very unevenly spaced. It hadn't been posted; it was handed to me by one of the footmen. I thought nothing of that at the time, for it's not so unusual for someone to send a note by hand, but later I questioned him as to where he obtained it. He said it was given to him at the door by a boy of the type often employed at inns to carry messages, and that this boy said he must give it to me when no one else was by.'

'I collect the footman did not know the boy? Or give you a description of him?'

46

She shook her head. 'Neither. I asked him too if the boy had said who had employed him on this errand, but John – the footman – had not thought to ask. I didn't pursue the matter too closely for the last thing I wanted was to set the servants gossiping.'

'And for that same reason, doubtless you'd prefer that I did not personally question your footman? Have no fear, I shall not do so. I doubt if there's anything to be learned there after this lapse of time. To return to the demand. How were you instructed to deliver the money?'

'I was to address it to a Mr Thompson and post it to the receiving office at Chancery Lane. It must arrive there by 15 March but, of course, I sent it off as soon as I managed to obtain the money, which was five days before that date. I didn't put it in with the rest of our mail but handed it to the postman myself,' she added with a shamefaced look. 'Oh, if only you could know how I have detested this odious deception!'

'I can imagine so, ma'am,' he replied gently. 'But perhaps the need for it will soon be at an end. If you will bear with me, there are one or two further points I'd like to examine. I collect you had some difficulty in raising the money? Would you care to tell me more of that?'

'When the letter came I was at my wits' end,' she said, clasping her hands in emotion. 'How was I to find such a sum? All my bills are paid by my husband, of course, and I have a quarterly allowance for pin-money, besides – most generous, I assure you! But it was toward the end of the quarter when I received that odious, horrible letter and I had only about one hundred pounds left. In the ordinary way I would only have to ask George for any sum, and he'd willingly give it me, but in this case I dared not. My brother was staying with us for a few days on his way to friends in Hertfordshire, so I asked him if he could make me a loan of four hundred pounds. He laughed, because his pockets are nearly always empty, and said why didn't I ask George.'

Justin nodded. 'That would seem reasonable enough, unless you confided in him?'

'Oh, no,' she said sadly. 'We've never been very close, alas. I had to tell him something, however, to account for my needing

47

the money, so I was obliged to let him think that I'd been gaming and was afraid to let George find out. He understood *that* well enough,' she went on with a tinge of bitterness in her voice, 'so he suggested I might pawn some of my jewellery. I could think of nothing but what had been given me by my husband – I could *never* bring myself to part with any of that! – but then at last I recollected a valuable old-fashioned necklace that mama had inherited from an aunt of hers and which she never wore because she disliked it. It came to me on mama's death and I had almost forgotten its existence. By the time I recollected it, my brother had departed, or else I could have asked him to transact the business for me.'

Justin reflected wryly that this was just as well. Judging by what he had learned of the lady's brother, she might have found herself somewhat light on the transaction.

'So you were obliged to set about it yourself,' was all he said. 'That must have been vastly disagreeable.'

She shuddered. 'Indeed it was! I couldn't think how to contrive, for I knew if I went to any of the fashionable jewellers it would be bound to come to my husband's ears. Then I hit upon the notion of asking one of the housemaids, who's a particular pet of mine, and she gave me the direction of an honest pawnbroker whom her family use sometimes. Only it was in such a low quarter, and that odious man must have seen me there, though I didn't see him, and then George came to hear of it, and he misunderstood – '

She broke off, close to tears.

Justin turned aside for a few moments, allowing Anthea to comfort and compose her friend.

'Pray don't distress yourself, ma'am,' he said presently in his quiet manner. 'The information you've given me will be of great value in solving the mystery of Yarnton's murder and in clearing George's name. I'd like you to promise that if ever you receive a second blackmail letter you'll bring it at once to me. Will you do that?'

She looked startled.

'A *second*? Do you think there will be others? Dear Heaven, I had hoped that this would be the end of it! Besides, how can I possibly find the means to meet any further demands?'

'I think it unlikely that the blackmailer will make any further application for some time, ma'am. He will no doubt have worked things out very carefully and realized that to press you too hard will spoil his game, because you'll be obliged to tell Velmond. But if such a demand is presented, you'll let me have it, will you not?'

She promised, incoherently but positively.

'Thank you. And if I may venture to offer a word of advice,' – the tone was diffident but his brown eyes were serious – 'it would be that you should conquer your fears and confide in George. He's a good fellow and I don't think you'll find him lacking in that sympathy and understanding which a wife expects of her husband. It would be of advantage if he and I could put our heads together over this affair, but obviously we can't do so until you decide to tell him. I'm bound by my promise to you to keep silent.'

Her eyes evaded his.

'Yes – yes – I see that, of course, but – I must have a little more time – it will not be easy – '

She broke off and extended her hand in farewell.

'You've been prodigiously kind, Mr Rutherford and I don't know how to thank you. I feel somewhat easier for having confided my troubles to you and your niece. I trust that in a happier time, if ever that comes, we may know each other better. Goodbye, and thank you – thank you!'

'So that's the position, Joe. We now know that Thompson was a blackmailer and that in some way Yarnton had smoked that fact out. What isn't so clear is whether Yarnton knew the actual identity of the blackmailer.'

'Well, one thing is clear, sir, if I may say so, and it's that if this Thompson heard deceased's remarks, we've got a strong motive for murder, stronger than Lord Velmond's.'

'True.' Justin frowned thoughtfully. 'Lady Quainton repeated to me the exact words used by Yarnton to the group of guests with her at the time. Those words were: 'I believe the gentleman in question is among us this evening, perhaps not so very far away?" Taken in conjunction with the fellow's previous question, what does that suggest to you, Joe?'

'That he definitely thought the blackmailer was one of that group, sir,' replied Watts promptly, 'though he may not have been sure which one.'

Justin nodded. 'I think it's a fair assumption. At any rate we can't afford to overlook it. There were nine people in that group, of whom four were ladies. We can discount them, of course.'

'A female wouldn't hardly have the strength to strangle a man,' agreed Watts.

'Nor, I believe, the temerity to enter the gentlemen's cloak-room,' said Justin drily. 'And that is where Yarnton was murdered. To resume. Of the five gentlemen we may rule out Velmond. Not simply because I believe him innocent, but more positively because it's palpably absurd to suppose him to be blackmailing his own wife. That leaves us with Cleveland, Bradfield, Dr Wetherby and Cleveland's secretary, Peyton.'

'We can count Mr Bradfield out, sir, can't we? We established that he was in the refreshment-room taking a drink with Lord Velmond until his lordship decided to leave. That hardly gives him more than ten minutes or so to get into the cloakroom ahead of his lordship, strangle his victim and make his escape. Not saying it couldn't be done, of course, if a man's cool and quick enough, but all the same – '

He shook his head doubtfully.

'Yes, it's unlikely, but I think we must include him in our investigations. We're going to need to look very carefully into the affairs and backgrounds of all these men. Fortunately, although I'm acquainted with them in a general way, none is a personal friend. I don't become involved with Town society to any extent, as I'm frequently either out of England or doing research in Oxford. I can therefore preserve a reasonable degree of detachment.'

'So what's our next move, sir?'

Justin brooded for a moment. 'Joe, when you made a search at Yarnton's rooms, did you chance to find any reference to Thompson among his papers? Of course, that name would mean nothing to you at the time, so you may not have noticed.'

Watts looked crestfallen. 'That's just it, sir. We did find a notebook, a sort of diary, y'know. We scanned through it, thinking to find some clue to his murderer there, but it wasn't no use. He'd written down all the bits of spying he'd done – very spiteful it was, sir – and several taunts he meant to throw at various individuals. We couldn't fathom who most of them were because he'd used initials or just one letter instead of a name. But nothing stood out, as you might say, and seeing as it was a dead bore to plough right through it, we gave it up. It's possible, though, that he may have mentioned Thompson, if only we'd known the name mattered and we'd troubled to go through the book more thoroughly.'

'What did you do with it?' demanded Justin, his eyes alight.

'Why, put it back in his bureau along of all his other papers. We locked the desk and kept the key, of course, and we locked up his rooms, too. Don't think his lawyer's been along so far to ask for the keys.'

'Splendid! We'll obtain them from Conant at once. I'd like to take a look at this diary myself.'

Chapter VI

The bookroom in Mr Henry Cleveland's house in St James's Square was situated at the front overlooking the gardens. It contained two writing desks, one for the Member of Parliament and a smaller one for his secretary. On a chilly, wet morning in late March the view through the window was not as pleasant as sometimes. Nevertheless, Cleveland stood looking out as one in a trance, the expression on his countenance matching the weather.

He drew a small notebook from his pocket, slowly turning the pages. Hearing a knock on the door he hastily restored it to its place, calling out permission to enter.

Roderick Peyton came in, looking the perfect secretary in his dark grey coat and trousers, his cravat tied in one of the more discreet styles.

'Good morning, sir,' he greeted Cleveland deferentially. 'I've opened the post and there are several letters requiring your personal attention. Mr Grey Bennet, who is to be chairman of the Select Parliamentary Committee on the Police, would like an appointment at your early convenience.'

'Yes. Well, consult my diary and see when I am free,' replied Cleveland somewhat absently.

He turned away from the window and sat down at his desk, pulling some papers towards him. Peyton also seated himself to begin work.

'Police,' said Cleveland thoughtfully. 'I wonder how Bow Street are progressing with the recent murder? Nasty business for Velmond.'

Peyton looked up. 'Yes, indeed. I have heard a rumour that his friend Mr Justin Rutherford is interesting himself in the case. Do you know if there's any truth in it, sir?'

Cleveland looked up sharply. 'Interesting himself? In what

way?'

'By what I heard, he was asking questions and had been to see the chief magistrate at Bow Street, Sir Nathaniel Conant.'

'You're vastly well informed,' said Cleveland, giving him a sharp glance.

'I try to keep my ear to the ground, sir,' replied Peyton modestly, 'in your interest.'

'Oh, yes, quite so. Well, young Rutherford is reputed to have a keen mind. If he interests himself in a subject I dare say he'll manage to master it.'

He picked up his pen with an air of finality. Peyton took the hint and settled to his own work.

Lucilla Velmond and Anthea had been doing a round of the fashionable shops again that morning, in spite of the inclement weather.

'For I simply must have some new gowns to wear now that the season is upon us,' said Anthea, sweeping Lucy before her into one of the foremost modiste's. 'And doubtless you'll wish to order something too.'

The proprietress of the establishment, a Mrs Banks who thought it professionally advantageous to call herself Madame Tufane, came quickly forward to greet this frequent and favoured customer. As she did so an assistant emerged from one of the cubicles escorting Mrs Cleveland, elegantly attired in a wine-coloured pelisse trimmed with fur and a matching bonnet.

'Why, how delightful to meet you!' exclaimed Mrs Cleveland in the gushing tones she reserved for female acquaintances. 'Are you bent on purchasing some new gowns? Lucky you, Miss Rutherford, since you have no husband to take you to task for extravagance. Mine has become a dead bore on the subject, I assure you! And of course you, Lady Velmond, have not yet been married long enough to incur that kind of reproach.'

A faint accent on the last part of her sentence brought a quick blush to Lucy's cheek.

'Isn't it atrocious weather,' said Anthea changing the subject quickly. 'We scarce knew whether to brave it and entertain

53

ourselves looking at fripperies, or remain within doors to watch the rain running down the window panes. But perhaps it will clear presently.'

'Indeed, I trust so, for I'm off tomorrow to Norfolk to see my daughter, Lady Barclay. She does not come up to Town, you know, so I must go to her occasionally.' She turned to Lucy. 'You will recollect Cecilia, will you not, Lady Velmond? You and she were schoolfellows in Bath, though I think you were never close friends.'

Lucy looked uncomfortable. 'Yes, we were at the same school. It's a long time ago now. How does Cecilia go on, ma'am? I trust she is well?'

'Oh, very well, thank you, though she is in' – she lowered her rather strident tones – 'a delicate condition just now. She was married last October to Sir Philip Barclay, who has an estate in Norfolk. I will remember you to her, shall I? I dare say she may recollect you,' she added in an offhand tone.

'Oh, yes, pray do so,' answered Lucy still a trifle ill at ease.

Mrs Cleveland parted from them and the serious business of the expedition began. But it was easy for Anthea to see that her companion's heart was not in the delightful creations of satin, silk and muslin in the fashionable pale shades which were paraded before them; so presently she took leave of Madame Tufane and escorted Lucy back to the waiting carriage.

They were both silent for a while as the conveyance bore them homewards. Then Anthea lightly touched her friend's hand.

'What is it, Lucy? Something has disturbed you, I know. Will you not tell me? It's to do with Mrs Cleveland's daughter, isn't it?'

Lucy nodded; a tear coursed its way down her cheek.

'It seems one can never leave behind the past,' she answered in a choking voice. 'I thought – I hoped and prayed – all that was over and done with years since! That girl – Cecilia Cleveland that was – she was never a friend of mine at school, but she knows all about, all about – '

She broke down. Anthea put an arm round her.

'About the reason why you received that blackmail letter, my love?' she finished for Lucy. 'Pray don't distress yourself. I dare say, whatever it is, she has long since forgotten it.'

Nevertheless Anthea made a mental note to inform Justin of this.

Later that day Runner Watts reported to Justin's rooms in Albemarle Street.

'No good,' he said gloomily. 'I questioned 'em all, but no one recalls a packet for Thompson, let alone anything about the bloke who collected it. It's a fiendish busy office that one, sir, with folk coming and going all day long.'

'No, I must admit I'd small hope at this interval of time, but we couldn't overlook the possibility. No matter, there may be other opportunities.' His tone changed. 'Did you bring the keys to Yarnton's place, Joe?'

Watts produced them.

'Good man. I think we'll postpone our visit there until dusk, though. Don't wish to set the neighbours in a bustle, do we?'

The dead man's servants had been paid off since their master's murder so the house had a slightly musty smell as they let themselves into the hall. Watts, who knew his way about from his previous visit, soon lit the candles in a branched candlestick on the hall table, carrying it with him to light their way.

'This is the room with the bureau where we found that diary, sir,' he said, pushing open a door on the right.

They entered, then stopped in their tracks, staring. A bureau bookcase stood against one wall and before it the floor was strewn with books and papers. The glass doors of the bookcase were flung wide and most of the books tumbled from the shelves. The lid of the bureau was lowered, revealing a jumble of papers which had spilled over on to the floor.

'Gawd's truth!' exclaimed Watts in dismay.

'I collect,' said Justin dryly, 'that this isn't quite as your people left it?'

'Gorblimey, us leave a ken in this state?' demanded Watts scornfully, lapsing into thieves' cant. 'Why, the guv'nor 'd have our lights an' liver for it, not arf he would!'

'Then someone else must have been here,' said Justin,

55

crossing over to the bureau and lifting up some of the loose papers. 'D'you know, Joe, I have the most melancholy persuasion that we shan't find that notebook here, after all.'

Watts shook his head in gloomy agreement.

'The keys never left Bow Street, so reckon it was a break-in,' he said. 'Let's take a look downstairs – sure to be in the basement.'

This proved to be accurate. They found a small window wide open. It looked out on to a yard and a gate leading to a narrow alley behind the houses, which eventually came out into the street.

Watts closed the window but found the catch was broken.

'Bust off, sir. We'll send round and get that mended tomorrow.

'Well, I suppose we may as well search for that notebook,' said Justin, as they returned to the burgled room. 'I dare say you'll want to check if anything else is missing, too. You'll have taken an inventory, I presume?'

Watts acknowledged that this had been done and produced his official notebook.

For the next hour, having lit all the candles in the room, they searched thoroughly; tidying all the contents of the desk and the litter surrounding it as they proceeded, but without finding the item they sought.

'Why pull out the books, I wonder?' mused Justin, as he stooped to retrieve two leatherbound volumes from the floor in order to restore them to the shelves. 'It suggests that our burglar didn't know precisely what he was seeking, wouldn't you say?'

'Well, come to that, sir, I don't rightly see how he could've done. Only Runner Grimshaw and me knew about the notebook – barring the guv'nor, that is – and even we didn't think it important at the time. If it was this here blackmailer, he was probably searching for anything that could give his game away – anything with the name Thompson on it.'

Justin nodded. 'Precisely my view. And it looks as if that notebook must have contained some reference of the kind. There's nothing else here that does – bills, receipts, a few letters, invitation cards, tradesmen's advertising material, coach timetables – pah!' he indicated the now reasonably tidy pigeon-holes of the bureau. 'What an unconscionable amount of paraphernalia we collect about us, Joe! And all to be bequeathed to an unappreciative posterity. It makes one wax philosophical, don't it?'

Rightly considering this to be a rhetorical question, Watts did not trouble to answer, but continued with the task which he had set himself after their fruitless search for the notebook. This was to check the other contents of the room against the inventory which had been taken on the Runners' first visit. After a second circuit of the room he looked up, frowning.

'Queer, sir, but I don't see this snuffbox anywhere hereabouts,' he said, tapping his notebook.

'Snuffbox? Have you a description of it?'

'Here, sir.' Watts indicated the item on the page.

'Gold and enamelled snuff box, oval, two and a quarter inches long, initials MY on base,' read Justin aloud.

'It was on this table, sir, by the snuff jar, which is still here. I've a good eye for positioning, sir, and I recollect that most particular.'

'It could easily have become swept off as our intruder moved around. The floor seems the most likely place.'

Together they searched the floor and all other possible hiding places for the snuffbox, but without success. Afterwards, they turned their attention to the route by which the burglar must have entered. At the end of a further hour Justin acknowledged defeat and abandoned the search. By that time his dark hair was completely dishevelled and his clothing, hands and face liberally streaked with dust.

'Good God!' he exclaimed, catching sight of himself in a mirror. 'I look for all the world like a road sweeper! Just as well it will be dark outside. I frequently look as bad when I'm grubbing around antiquities but I'm unlikely to encounter anyone of my acquaintance on such ploys. Is there a pump in the yard here, do you know? It's too much to hope there'll be water laid on to the house.'

Watts confirmed that there was indeed a pump, so they both went outside to remove the traces of grime as best they might, shuddering at the ice cold water.

'We'll leave by this back way, I think,' said Justin, as he rubbed himself dry on a towel they had found in one of the kitchen drawers. 'We'll attract less notice. Queer thing about that snuffbox – almost leads one to suppose our intruder was a professional burglar, except that objects of greater value were left. Now what d'you suppose he could have wanted with it?' A thought struck him. 'Did you look inside?'

'No, sir, but if you're thinking it might've held something instead of snuff, you'd catch cold on that, I opine. The box wasn't above an inch deep, a bit less, I'd say.'

Justin nodded. 'The usual size. All the same, possibly it could contain a scrap of paper – just a thought, I'll admit not perhaps a prodigiously inspired one. Come on, then. Let's be off.'

They emerged stealthily from the back door of the premises, locking it behind them, then stood still for a few moments to let their eyes become accustomed to the gloom. By now it was dark but a faint glimmer of light came from a fitful moon. They trod quietly across the yard and through the gate into the alley. It was too narrow for them to walk comfortably side by side, so they went in single file, Watts leading the way.

They had traversed more than half the distance which led to the street beyond when, without warning, two figures armed with stout cudgels sprang from the shadow of a gateway.

One launched himself upon Watts, cudgel raised. The Runner was quick to draw his official truncheon to parry the first blow. Meanwhile the second turned his attention to Justin, who was unarmed.

If he had thought to find an easy prey, the assailant soon found his mistake. Dodging a stroke from the cudgel Justin slammed home a hefty punch to the jaw, which made his attacker pause momentarily. Justin seized his advantage by rushing in to butt the other man in the chest and wrest the weapon from his hand. Seeing the tables were now turned the attacker did not stay to try conclusions but fled, thrusting the other two struggling figures aside in his passage.

Justin started in pursuit but stopped abruptly on seeing that Watts had fallen to the ground and his attacker was about to bring his cudgel down on the helpless Runner's head. Seizing the man's arm he tussled with him for possession of the weapon, while Watts still lay inert. The attacker was a burly fellow; but for all his slender build, Justin's muscles were in good trim so the honours were more even than might have been supposed. He had just succeeded in knocking the cudgel from the other's hold when Watts joined the fray, having recovered from his temporary unconsciousness. A blow from his truncheon felled the man, who lay like one dead.

The two companions leaned against the wall, panting.

'You all right, Joe?' asked Justin breathlessly.

'Aye, right enough, though I reckon I'll have a bruise or two. Knocked me cold for a moment, yon bastard.'

Justin looked down at the inert figure at their feet.

'Hope to God you haven't killed him.'

'No more'n his deserts.' Watts turned the man over face upwards. 'Reckon I know his ugly mug, too,' he said thoughtfully. 'Can't put a name to it, offhand, but one o' these bully boys who hang around the flash houses, I'll swear.'

Justin knew that the term 'flash house' was applied to the lower type of tavern where thieves commonly met. It was not unusual, either, for the Runners to frequent such places in search of information.

'What d'you mean to do with him?'

'Take him in, see if we can get anything out of him. Do you stay by him, sir,' Watts instructed, handing over his truncheon to Justin, 'while I get a hackney to take him off to Bow Street.'

Justin nodded but thrust the truncheon aside.

'I'll manage without that.'

Watts grinned. 'Reckon you will, sir. You pack a handy bunch o' fives.'

'Give the credit to Gentleman Jackson, although it's some time since last I sparred with him. I'd best look in again at his boxing academy in Old Bond Street if we're to have much of this sort of ploy, though. Now, I wonder, Joe, did these two set upon us by chance or was there more to it than that?'

*A*t well past midnight the atmosphere inside the Magpie and Stump in Skinner Street would not have suited a fastidious man. Compounded of the odours of unwashed clothing and bodies, filthy sawdust-strewn floors, cheap raw liquor, the smoke from clay pipes filled with rank tobacco, not to mention the stench caused by the unhygienic habits of the tavern's customers, it assailed even accustomed nostrils powerfully. But in the course of duty Joseph Watts had frequently been obliged to patronize this and other of the flash houses; so although a slight spasm crossed his features as he entered, he managed to control his inner feelings of disgust.

Although he had taken care to dress in his oldest clothes, he still presented a more respectable appearance than most other customers. Though many of these were too busy about their own concerns of drinking and whoring, some few looked at him askance, recognizing him for what he was. With a quick motion of his head, he summoned one of these to his side.

The fellow looked reluctant but at last approached, thrusting aside with a curse the individuals who stood in his way.

'Want a word,' said Watts briefly. 'Outside.'

The other protested that it was cold outside and moreover there was nothing to warm a cove out there.

'Take some of your blue ruin with you,' replied Watts, surreptitiously sliding a coin into the other's hand, for it would never do to be flashing money around here. 'No, not for me – my guts won't take it.'

The man obtained his beverage after a wordy struggle with others of a like mind, drained half of it, then joined Watts in a second fight, this time to reach the door.

'Gawd's truth!' gasped the Runner, when he once more stood in the far from fresh, but slightly less foetid air of Skinner Street.

'What a stinking hole!'

He led the way round the corner of the tavern to a neglected yard which was deserted at present. Here he halted in the partial shelter of a lean-to structure against one wall of the building.

The other man stopped also, facing him warily.

'Whad yer want wi' me? I ain't done nuffink.'

'That'll be the day,' said Watts sceptically. 'Bill Flitch is in custody. He mentioned your name – said you'd brought a message to him and to another cove we've not laid by the heels yet. We want to know who gave you this here message.'

'Flitch!' The other spat expressively. 'Don't yer go for believin' anythink 'e says, bloody liar, 'e is.'

'Like his mates,' agreed Watts. 'Only this time, I reckon he's telling the truth for once. Come on, Sims, let's be knowing – and don't say you've forgotten,' – as he saw the excuse forming on the other man's lips – 'or else I might start recollecting a few things about you that *I've* conveniently forgotten.'

'Dunno who this cove was, an' that's Gawd's truth,' said Sims, rapidly changing his mind as to tactics. 'Never set eyes on 'im afore. Come in 'ere a coupla nights back, asks for me, says 'e needs a coupla bully lads to do a job. Dunno 'ow 'e knows me moniker, so no use askin',' he added for good measure.

'Word gets round that you're a fixer, that's for sure. So you'd never seen this man before? What was he like?'

Sims shrugged. 'Dunno – 'e didn't stay more'n coupla minutes, an' kep' out o' the light. Not much light, best o' times.'

This was true enough. The Magpie and Stump catered for those who preferred the anonymity of gloom.

'Still, you must have seen enough to get some notion of his looks. How old? Tall or short? Fat or thin? Colouring? Come on, man!'

'Not rightly old, nor young,' said Sims, pondering these queries. 'Belly on 'im, though. Whiskers – 'bout as tall as me.'

'Medium height, then. What d'you mean by whiskers? Beard? Sideburns?'

'Nah, more like 'e 'adn't shaved for a week or so.'

'What colour hair, then?'

'Gawd, I dunno,' replied Sims despairingly. 'Look, mister,

it's bloody cold 'ere, an' I've telt yer all I knows. Lemme go now.'

'In a minute. What manner of voice?'

'Like other folks.'

'You mean he spoke just as you and your mates do?'

Sims considered this. 'Mostly,' he pronounced at last. 'Coupla times, more like yer do. Wasn't yer, was it?' he asked with an attempt at humour.

'I'll tell you this much,' said Watts, unamused. 'Better watch your step or you'll hear more of my voice than you'll relish. On your way, then.'

Justin had been dining with his eldest brother, Viscount Rutherford, and his family at their town house in Berkeley Square. After dinner Lady Rutherford and Anthea had been escorted to Almack's by one of Anthea's many admirers, Justin resisting all his niece's attempts to persuade him to make one of their party.

'You know Almack's ain't much in my line, my dear girl,' he said to her *sotto voce*. 'Besides, I particularly wish to talk to Ned privately.'

She pouted. 'So you've no further use for me as a confederate now. I see. How like a male, to obtain all the aid possible from a female and then abandon her. But don't suppose you'll escape me this lightly, monster! I mean to know everything you've been doing and all you've discovered – only wait until I get you alone next time!'

'It's a pleasure I scarce know how to postpone, ma'am. But you mustn't keep your escort waiting – the poor devil will be counting the minutes and turning them into hours. No, no,' – as she showed signs of protesting – 'I promise I'll recount the whole eventually but you must allow me time to set my theories and discoveries in some sort of order.'

She accepted this, bestowed a brilliant smile upon him in reward and followed her mama from the room.

'You injured your arm, Justin?' demanded Edward as he watched his brother pour the wine. 'Noticed something at dinner but naturally didn't mention it in front of the females.'

'Nothing much, a slight stiffness merely, from bruising. Tried conclusions with a couple of footpads the other evening.'

Edward raised his eyebrows. 'Footpads, eh? Whereabouts? Did they get anything from you?'

'Only a thick head – one of 'em at least. The other got away but he'll be laid by the heels soon enough, so Runner Watts assures me.'

Edward looked disturbed. 'Just what are you about, old fellow? Consorting with Bow Street Runners – '

'Joe Watts is my erstwhile companion from my time with Wellington. He joined Bow Street on his discharge. I've hired him to aid me in my investigations into Yarnton's murder.'

'Yes, I'd heard a rumour that you're concerning yourself in that business. For God's sake, Justin, why must you be always up to these freakish starts?' demanded Edward in a pained tone. 'Take my advice and leave it to the authorities. Why the devil you can't content yourself with the normal sporting activities of a gentleman when you feel the need for a change from academic pursuits is more than I can fathom! But so it's always been!'

'Unregenerate character, ain't I?' said Justin with a grin. 'But it's of interest to learn that someone's got wind of my involvement in this affair. Where did you hear this rumour, Ned?'

'Can't rightly say – someone at White's I think. I wasn't best pleased, as you may know, so I damn well brushed the topic aside quickly. What's it all about, old chap? I know Velmond's supposed to be under suspicion – damn ridiculous of course!'

'Not now, I think. But I'll tell you the whole – in return for some information I need from you.'

Lord Rutherford stared. 'Don't know what *I* can tell you. But fire away then.'

Justin sipped his wine before replying. 'Don't need to say, I suppose,' he began, 'that you must keep your mouth shut?'

Edward nodded.

'The truth is, then, that Yarnton was murdered because he was foolhardy enough to direct one of his notorious taunts at a blackmailer.'

'Good God, a *blackmailer*! What in thunder are things coming to? A blackmailer circulating among the *ton*! Have you any notion who it may be?''

Justin shook his head. 'Not for certain, though I have narrowed the possibilities down to a short list of suspects. Let me explain.'

He outlined briefly the information he possessed and his deductions from it. His brother listened attentively, a shocked expression on his face.

'So you see there are four men – Cleveland, his secretary, Bradfield and Dr Wetherby – any one of whom could be the guilty party. I've no more than a nodding acquaintance with any of 'em, and I've never set eyes on Peyton, the secretary, at all. I'd like you to tell me what you know about them. Start with the MP, Cleveland.'

'Cleveland? He's a Tory and opposed to any kind of reform like the rest of the party. Not much else to say about him. He don't make much stir in the House, not one of your up-and-coming politicians.'

'Has he any particular friends in the House?'

Edward considered this for a moment. 'He was pretty thick with Cochrane at one time. You remember, the fellow who was convicted of fraud in the Stock Exchange case two years ago. In fact, one or two people wondered at the time if Cleveland himself was involved but he was never charged so there couldn't have been any evidence.'

'Extraordinary case, that,' agreed Justin. 'I wasn't in England at that time but I collect that it depended upon play-acting by a group of adventurers.'

Edward nodded. 'That's so. A man named de Béranger dressed up in military costume and presented false reports about the overthrow of Napoleon in France to the Port Admiral of Deal. His intention was that the false intelligence should be forwarded to London by the semaphore telegraph but fog prevented this, so instead he posted to Lord Cochrane's house with it. When the news reached the Stock Exchange, Omniums and Consuls soared of course. Three other bogus officers followed to give the rumours a further boost. The conspirators had previously acquired large holdings of the stock and they sold it at the inflated price. A month later, after the news was proved to be false, the Stock Exchange held an inquiry. Cochrane and his brother were in it up to their necks.'

'Hm. Well, if Cleveland did make anything out of it, presumably he's in easy circumstances.'

'I'm not so sure of that. There've been rumours lately that he's selling off his stable and cutting down on domestic staff. Mrs Cleveland's extravagant, by what the females say, somewhat beyond the normal for womenkind. All this is gossip, of course,' he added hastily, 'so don't refine too much upon it.'

'No smoke without fire all the same. A man in financial straits is more likely to turn to blackmail than one who's plump in the pocket, wouldn't you say?'

Viscount Rutherford agreed uneasily. 'But a man in his position would be taking a devilish risk.'

'True. I believe there's a daughter?'

'Yes, that's right. She came out last year and shortly afterwards married a man with an estate in Norfolk.'

'I collect that at one time the Clevelands lived in Somerset and that their daughter attended a young ladies' seminary in Bath?'

Edward nodded. 'They came to live in Town after Cleveland got his seat, about six years ago. They left the girl at school in Bath until last year, so m' wife told me.'

'It might interest you to know, Ned, that Cleveland's daughter attended the same school as Velmond's wife. Also that the indiscretion for which Lady Velmond is now being blackmailed occurred while she was at the seminary.'

'Good God! Do you mean to suggest – ?'

'It's a possibility that I can't afford to overlook, at all events.'

'I can't credit it!' exclaimed Edward in a horrified tone. 'A man in his position! But you say this blackmail demand arrived recently, and it was the first,' he added thoughtfully. 'Presumably Lucilla Velmond's, ah, indiscretion, whatever it may be, occurred some years back, so why wait until now?'

'Dear me, Ned, I fear you'd never make a detective,' said Justin, pityingly. 'Don't you see, old chap, it's only now that poor little Lucilla has wed a rich man? Until then, she was the daughter of an impoverished squire.'

'I tell you what, Justin, this is a damnably unpleasant

business! I only hope you're not making a mistake or there'll be the devil to pay and no pitch hot!'

'Ah, but we mustn't jump to conclusions,' put in Justin, wagging a cautionary finger. 'So far this is all *theory*, understand? It remains to be proved. Now let's consider the other candidates. What do you know about Cleveland's secretary for example?'

Edward looked relieved at this change of focus.

'Peyton? Not much. Handsome young fellow of about four and twenty. He's a distant relative of Mrs Cleveland and she persuaded her husband to offer the boy this post when he came down from Cambridge a few years since. Family not too well off I collect, so couldn't do much for him. Seems to discharge his duties conscientiously enough. Don't know anything about his private life, as naturally he don't mix in our circles.'

'Does his family reside in Somerset too?'

'No, I believe it's Hertfordshire or Buckingham, not far from Town. Dare say Eliza could tell you for certain, if it matters. She knows all the gossip, like most matrons bless 'em.'

'Perhaps I ought to have applied to my sister-in-law instead of you,' agreed Justin laughing. 'I should mention that Anthea's been of prodigious help to me already – but for her I should most likely not have learned of Lady Velmond's blackmail.'

Edward frowned. 'See here, my boy, not sure I care for that. Anthea's a resty chit – takes after you more than she does after her mother or myself – and there's no saying what starts she'll get up to if once you let her have her head. Seems to me this affair could be dangerous. Yarnton murdered, and yourself attacked. You don't say outright that the footpads were set on you by someone else, but I'm not quite a fool, y'know.'

'Don't worry, I'll keep her out of anything risky. In fact it's unlikely that I'll need to ask for her help again.'

'You may get it, whether you will or no,' Edward warned him. 'No holding the chit once she's got the bit between her teeth! I'll hold you accountable for her safety, and don't forget it.'

'I won't. I value my niece highly, Ned, I assure you. But to resume – what d'you know of Bradfield?'

'Ask Velmond. He's one of George's set. Not a bad crowd on the whole. None of 'em go in for deep play or expensive lightskirts, and that's saying a lot these days.'

Justin chuckled. 'That's your Scots Presbyterian blood showing, old chap! But I won't roast you on that subject. Is Bradfield married? Does he reside in Town, do you know?'

'Yes, he's married with young children and his country estate's in Sussex. His wife's there most of the time. I collect she doesn't like London.'

'Any financial difficulties?'

'Shouldn't think so, but perhaps George Velmond could tell you. By the way, Justin, does Velmond know about this business with his wife?'

'Not unless she's told him by now. I did my best to persuade her to it, but I've reason to believe that so far she hasn't followed my advice. Foolish, but understandable I suppose. I pledged myself to secrecy.'

'Awkward. It means you can't confide your suspicions to him.' He paused, then asked, 'Whatever can the foolish child have done to lay herself open to extortion? She seems such an innocent little creature.'

'I think she is and that may have been the cause of her indiscretion. I've no notion what it was. If she told Anthea, my niece didn't see fit to pass it on to me.'

'Hang together, females. But so do we after all.'

Justin nodded. 'Self-preservation of the sexes. Well, you can't tell me much about Bradfield, Ned, so I'll have to try elsewhere. What about Dr Wetherby?'

'Oh, it couldn't be Wetherby,' replied his brother confidently. 'Doing very well for himself, has been these ten years. He's in and out of all the *ton* households and not only as a medico, mark you. He's invited to social occasions too. Has a good house in Bruton Street, keeps a tolerable stable with a couple of carriages – none of your doctor's modest gigs for Wetherby! He's been attending my household for some years now and that of almost everyone I know. He's very much relied upon – sound medical man.'

'Married?'

'No, a widower. His wife died three or four years back.

There's no family.'

'Seems to me,' said Justin thoughtfully, 'a man in his position would have access to a good many personal secrets. The sickroom, y' know, is pretty much a confessional chamber.'

'Aye, but I can't see Wetherby going in for blackmail, though. His pockets are well enough lined as it is. He'd be a fool to jeopardize a highly successful career for the sake of a paltry sum like — what did you say the amount was?'

'Five hundred pounds,' supplied Justin.

'Well, I ask you! Ridiculous!'

'Perhaps so, if that were all.'

'All? What d'you mean? I don't follow you.'

'Simply, my dear Ned, that for anything I know at present, there may be other blackmail victims.'

Chapter VIII

On the following morning Justin decided to look in at White's in the hope of gleaning further information concerning his principal suspects. He encountered Velmond there. The two had not met during the past week and Justin was taken aback to notice that his friend showed all the signs of a man who had been drinking heavily in the interval.

'You're the very chap I want to see,' declared Velmond in slightly slurred accents. 'You found out yet who this scoundrel T – '

He had not troubled to lower his voice but stopped abruptly as Justin took his arm in a hard grip.

'Wassermatter?' he protested. 'I only wanted to ask you – '

'Yes, I know what you want,' said Justin quietly. 'But first let's find a more secluded spot, what?'

Keeping his hold on Velmond's arm, he steered his friend into another room which was unoccupied except for three elderly gentlemen quietly snoozing behind their newspapers. He chose a couple of seats at a small table removed at some distance from these and beckoned a waiter.

'Join me in a bottle?' asked Velmond.

'No, not at present thank you. Coffee, I think – black as hell.'

Velmond shrugged but made no protest, drinking the coffee gratefully enough when it arrived.

'Rather think I needed that,' he said, more in his normal tones.

'Been hitting the bottle, George? Not like you.'

'Well, what's a fellow to do?' demanded Velmond defensively. 'If your wife had been conducting an affaire with someone else – '

'She hasn't,' interrupted Justin with emphasis.

Velmond's expression changed and he leaned forward

eagerly. 'You're sure of that, Justin? How d'you know? For God's sake, tell me at once!'

Justin shook his head. 'Afraid I can't, old chap. You must ask Lady Velmond yourself. But I give you my word that there's nothing of that kind.'

'Devil take it, man, you can't leave matters in the air in that fashion! How do I know that you ain't just fobbing me off?'

'Because I hope you know me better than that. There are good reasons why I can't explain fully, but you may take my word for it that your wife is completely innocent of the charge you've laid upon her. Only ask her, George.'

'Easier said than done,' muttered Velmond. 'There's been a coolness between us ever since I first taxed her with it. We've scarce spoken a word to each other since then. I've been spending most of my time either here or at Brooks's.'

Justin said nothing to this, feeling as though he were treading on eggshells. Velmond was also silent for a while, brooding. Presently he roused himself.

'What of this man Thompson, then?' he demanded. 'Where does he come into it, if he's not Lucy's lover?'

'Unless I'm much mistaken, he's Yarnton's murderer.'

Velmond stared. Justin was silent for a moment, wondering how to disclose some of the information he possessed without involving Lucilla Velmond.

'But I don't see that,' objected Velmond. 'As far as I know there was no one called by that name present at the soirée.'

'It's a pseudonym. I believe that Yarnton had discovered who Thompson really was and was taunting the man in his customary style. A taunt that was answered with murder.'

'Good God! You mean there was some scandal that one of the guests feared to have made public and that he was prepared to kill to protect his secret? But that means – devil take it, I'm acquainted with the majority of those who were present! It's monstrous!'

'More monstrous than believing your wife to be unfaithful to you?'

'Well, no, not so, of course! But how can you be so positive, Justin?'

'I've done a certain amount of investigation, aided by

70

Runner Watts. I'd prefer you not to press me for details now though, old fellow, because I've still a long way to go before I can definitely put my finger on the culprit. Moreover, if I breathe my suspicions to you, ten to one you'll give the game away by acting oddly with the suspects. You're too honest for the subterfuge necessary in detection, I fear.'

'Well, I can't pretend to regret that,' said George in downright tones. 'I do see your point though and perhaps it would be best if I don't know too much. All that matters to me, after all, is that Lucy should be innocent!'

'I imagine,' said Justin dryly, 'that it also matters marginally that you should be cleared of any suspicion as Yarnton's murderer?'

'That, of course. But I may tell you the other matter has far outweighed that recently. All the same, my dear chap, I'm devilish grateful to you for all your efforts on my behalf. Come and dine with us soon, will you?'

'There's a person asking to see you, sir.'

Henry Cleveland looked up from his writing, an impatient frown on his face.

'A person? What do you mean by that, Gibbs?'

The butler looked crestfallen. He hardly knew how to describe the caller otherwise.

'An official, Mr Cleveland, a Bow Street Runner named Watts. Very insistent he is, although I told him, of course, that all appointments should be made through Mr Peyton.'

He gestured diffidently towards the secretary, who had also paused in his work, looking up attentively. Peyton rose from his desk.

'Shall I deal with him for you, sir? Some routine matter, doubtless, that you need not be troubled with.'

'I beg your pardon, Mr Peyton,' interposed Gibbs apologetically. 'I have already intimated as much to the Bow Street man but he insists on seeing Mr Cleveland in person. What are your instructions, sir?' he added, looking doubtfully at his master.

Cleveland threw down his pen irritably. 'Oh, very well, show him in,' he ordered. 'But if there's much more of this kind of thing I intend to lodge a strong complaint with the Home Secretary. Anyone would suppose this to be a police state after the manner of France.'

He glared coldly at Watts when the Runner was admitted. Peyton tactfully rose to quit the room but was waved back to his seat by his employer.

'To what do I owe this intrusion?' asked Cleveland brusquely.

'Just a little matter in pursuit of our investigations into the murder of Marmaduke Yarnton, sir,' began Watts in a respectful but firm tone. 'If you would be so good as to answer a question or two?'

'I consider that I've already answered questions enough,' said the politician frigidly. 'Sir Nathaniel Conant seemed satisfied at the time.'

'With respect, sir, there's a question which wasn't put when we carried out our original interrogation.' Watts was standing to attention in his old army style, his hat held beneath one arm. 'It has become of interest since then.'

Cleveland made an impatient gesture.

'Very well, ask it, my good man. Pray be brief for my time is valuable, as you may perhaps know,' he added dryly.

'Yessir. It's this – does the name Thompson mean anything to you, sir?'

He rapped out the question smartly so as not to give warning of what was coming.

If he had hoped to produce any reaction in either of his auditors – and he had carefully positioned himself so that both were under his eye – he was to be disappointed.

Cleveland gave a long-suffering sigh.

'Should it?' he demanded plaintively. 'It's a common enough name, I suppose. One of my constituents perhaps? Though what connection it can possibly have with your investigations, is, I must confess, quite beyond my comprehension.'

'If I might prompt your memory, sir, deceased put much the same question to a group of guests on the evening of his murder. He seemed to think that someone in that group knew who this Thompson was. We would like to know too, sir.'

Cleveland frowned as if in an effort of recollection.

'Did he? Oh, yes, I rather think he did make some cryptic reference to that name. But then he was addicted to cryptic remarks, you know. I would advise you not to refine too much upon it.'

'So you don't know who Thompson is, sir?' persisted Watts.

'No, I do not. And now, if you've quite finished, I'd like to be allowed to continue with my work. Reasonable co-operation with Bow Street I will always be prepared to offer, of course, but this I consider to be the outside of enough.'

When Watts had gone Roderick Peyton looked interrogatively at his employer.

'It would seem, sir, that Bow Street no longer suspects Lord Velmond of the murder.'

'One cannot say. Naturally it's their duty to cast around and examine other possibilities, since there is insufficient evidence so far to secure a conviction.' He frowned. 'One wonders why their attention should have been drawn to that particular remark of Yarnton's, all the same. As I pointed out, the fellow made so many remarks of the kind, calculated to annoy or embarrass his hearers. This one seemed to me to have neither more nor less purpose than a score of others I've heard him make.'

'It is interesting to have your views on that head, Mr Cleveland,' Peyton said deferentially. 'I must admit that the impression left on me by the remark at the time was of its being extremely pointed – tantamount to an accusation in fact. But then, I was never before in company with the dead man, although I knew of his reputation, so I must consider you to be the superior judge, sir.'

'Hm. Well, enough time has been wasted on the subject,' said Cleveland peremptorily. 'Tell me, have I any appointments for the remainder of the day?'

Peyton consulted his desk diary.

'No, sir, nothing until tomorrow at eleven o' clock, when you have an appointment with Mr Grey Bennet, whom you may recall – '

'Yes, yes,' interrupted Cleveland impatiently. 'The Committee on the Police. I take it you've prepared a brief for me?'

'Oh, yes, Mr Cleveland,' replied Peyton with just a shade of reproach in his tone.

'Of course, you're a good fellow, Peyton. Well, since there's nothing to detain me here, I have a little outside business to attend to. I'll see you later.'

He crossed to the bell pull and ordered his curricle to the door. Presently he was driving along the crowded Strand and into Fleet Street. For once the morning was fine so he left his vehicle at the Cock tavern and walked by way of Chancery Lane and Carey Street into the pleasant green of Lincoln's Inn Fields.

Here he knocked upon the door of one of the houses surrounding the square and was at once admitted by an earnest young clerk to an office on the ground floor.

He never noticed that his perambulations had been followed by that same tiresome individual who had interviewed him earlier.

At about much the same time Justin was seated opposite Dr Wetherby in the latter's opulent consulting-rooms in Harley Street. Everything about the apartment spoke of good taste and affluence, from the thick Aubusson carpet underfoot to the ormolu clock supported by cherubs which stood on the marble mantelshelf.

'I collect you do not wish to consult me about your health, Mr Rutherford,' said the doctor in his measured tones but with an ingratiating smile.

'No, nothing of that kind,' replied Justin. 'I'm happy to say that my health is of the rudest. For the benefit of those who may not be so fortunate, I promise not to take up too much of your valuable time.'

'Not at all.' Wetherby's manner grew more expansive. 'I have had the privilege of ministering to Viscount Rutherford's household for some years now and deem it an honour to meet a member of that family as distinguished in the academic field as yourself.'

Justin bowed. 'It is good of you to say so, doctor. A gentleman in your profession encounters a wider circle of acquaintance than most men, I think?'

The doctor nodded, his shrewd eyes studying his guest.

'That is so, Mr Rutherford. Pray tell me if there is any way in which my knowledge might serve you.'

'I'll answer your question in the Scottish fashion, by asking another,' said Justin smiling. 'Do you recollect the remarks passed by the unfortunate Yarnton on the evening of his murder – remarks concerning a certain Mr Thompson?'

The doctor's eyes narrowed. 'Ah, yes,' he replied slowly.

'Reports suggest that he appeared to be convinced that one of his auditors was quite aware of the mysterious Thompson's identity. May I ask if his remarks struck you in that light?'

Dr Wetherby paused for a moment, evidently recapitulating in his mind what had passed. Finally he nodded.

'Yes, I would say so. But Yarnton was an extraordinary character, you know. I mean that in the true significance of the word – out of the ordinary.' A little of the lecture theatre manner crept into his voice. 'There are men who seek to draw attention to themselves by sartorial elegance, such as Mr Brummell, whose star, alas, is no longer in the ascendant. There are those who cultivate eccentricities of behaviour, such as Mr Byng, whose habit it is to drive about with a poodle up beside him in his curricle. With the unfortunate Mr Yarnton it was a more objectionable form of exhibitionism. I need not expatiate, for you are well aware, my dear sir, of his particular weakness – fatal, as it turned out in the end.'

'Of course.' Justin tried not to show the boredom which understandably crept over him. 'I collect that you, too, are of the opinion, doctor, that Yarnton was murdered because of his mention of the name Thompson?'

Wetherby placed his fingers together in a judicial attitude.

'Ah. As to that, possibly one could be mistaken,' he said carefully. 'Certainly it would appear that one or another of his malicious remarks brought retribution in its train. Inquiry has so far established no other possible motive.'

'Exactly. And for my money, this reference to Thompson wins hands down,' replied Justin, flippantly. 'Now, sir, may I ask you if you happen to know anyone of that name – say among your patients?'

There was a longer pause than usual. Evidently Dr

Wetherby, like most members of his profession, was in the habit of considering his words carefully.

'It is some years since I attended any patient with such an undistinguished name,' he said at last. 'You may be aware, Mr Rutherford, that I have the honour to attend some of the foremost members of the *ton*, not least among whom is your own respected family.' Here he gave a little bow. 'When I walked the wards at Guy's, however,' – with a shrug – 'there may have been a Thompson, just as surely as there were Browns, Smiths, Greens and others of similarly humble names. I can only say that I have no clear recollection of any such at this distance in time.'

Justin nodded. 'I see.' He leaned forward and shot out the next question abruptly. 'And you have no notion whom Yarnton was baiting of those among your group?'

Did he detect the faintest flicker of awareness in those shrewd, steel grey eyes? If so it was gone in a moment.

Dr Wetherby shook his head.

'None whatsoever,' he answered steadily.

Chapter IX

Try as she might to nerve herself for the task, Lucy could not find the courage to confess the truth to her husband. Ever since that day when he had accused her of being unfaithful to him, he had treated her with coldness and reserve. He was seldom at home and even when he was, showed no inclination for her company. Had it not been for Anthea Rutherford's friendship she would indeed have been lonely and miserable. There are some things, however, which a married woman is reluctant to confide to a spinster friend; so although Anthea knew that Lucy had not so far unburdened herself to her husband, she had no notion how very wide the rift between them had grown. In consequence she kept urging Lucy to tell Velmond the truth and secretly feeling a trifle impatient with her friend for shrinking from this.

'But your own husband!' she exclaimed on the last of these occasions. 'Since yours is a lovematch, surely there can be no doubt that he will understand and forgive? The past is over and done with, Lucy – it's the present which matters. You must surely see that. And it's much wiser to tell him yourself, for then this fiendish blackmailer will have no further hold over you.'

'I know you are right,' said Lucy weakly, 'but indeed, Anthea, it is not so simple as you suppose. I must choose a suitable moment and there never seems to be one lately. It would be easier if I did not care for him so much,' she went on in a desperate tone, 'for then I would not fear so greatly to lose his affection – if, indeed, I haven't already done so! Oh, pray do not tease me on this subject, dearest Anthea!'

At that Anthea desisted, doing her best not to bring up the subject again.

On the morning that Velmond had encountered Justin in White's the two girls had been out driving together and Anthea had been obliged to return home for an afternoon engagement, leaving Lucy to eat a solitary nuncheon. She was toying with a little cold meat and fruit for which she had no appetite, when Velmond burst into the morning-room, where the meal had been served on a tray.

One startled look at his face told her that he was in a very different frame of mind from latterly. She half rose from her chair and he clasped her in a warm embrace.

'Lucy, dearest! I was hoping to find you alone. There's so much I want to say – but I'm interrupting your meal,' he continued, a little disappointed that she did not respond at once to his ardent greeting. 'I'll join you. We'll ring for some more provender, shall we?'

He pulled the bell rope, while she did her best to compose a welter of conflicting emotions within her. It was wonderful to see once more the love in his eyes but how could she reciprocate as she would have wished with this dreadful weight still on her conscience? How much did he know? Could it be that Mr Rutherford had broken his promise to her and revealed her secret? Almost she hoped that this had happened, for then she would be relieved of the painful necessity of explaining matters herself.

The necessary interlude while the servants came and went did little to put her thoughts in order. She concentrated hard on practicalities, helping Velmond to food and trying to look as if she herself wanted to continue with the meal.

'Didn't realize I was so sharp set,' he said, having speedily done justice to a large plateful of ham and beef and ignoring the wine which the butler had thoughtfully provided. 'Have you quite finished, my love? Won't you take some of this fruit? No? 'Pon my word, you don't eat enough to keep a gnat alive! However, if you're quite sure, we'll have this cleared away and then enjoy a quiet little cose together on the sofa.'

It was a prospect which would have delighted Lucilla at one time but which now filled her with alarm. In desperation she glanced at the clock.

'I – I'm afraid I'm obliged to go out again in a little while,' she said timidly.

His face clouded. 'So soon? Cannot it be put off, my love?'

'Well, I, the thing is, I'm due at Madame Tufane's for a final fitting for my new evening gown. But, of course, if you wish me to stay – '

'Oh, no, no such thing,' he said hastily, not wanting to be selfish. 'A new evening gown is more important than a chat to me – we can talk together at any time, after all. Besides, you will wish to have the gown ready for a small dinner party I mean to give on Saturday. It's time we began entertaining, don't you think?'

'Who will be coming?' she asked, seizing on this welcome change of topic.

'The Rutherfords, of course, Bradfield and a few others of my close friends. Also anyone you may care to invite, naturally.'

'Then perhaps Lady Quainton?' suggested Lucy diffidently. 'She has been so very good to me.'

'By all means,' he answered expansively, rising from the table and coming over to her chair. 'Lucy, I mustn't detain you now, I know, but I wish to apologize – humbly – for the unworthy suspicions I've been entertaining of you recently! How I could have been such a poor, deluded fool as not to realize that I could trust implicitly in your integrity – oh, what can I say to mend matters? Put it down, dearest girl, to my insane jealousy. Forgive me if you can, this once, and I promise never to err again! Only say you can forgive me, Lucy!'

She stood up, her knees trembling under her, and faced him with tears brimming her eyes.

'Forgive *you*?' she stammered, scarcely knowing what she said. 'Oh, George, it is you who must forgive *me*! You don't know – '

He placed a tender, protective arm about her.

'There, now I've upset you, brute that I am,' he said gently. 'Run along to your appointment now and we'll talk later. That is, if you wish.'

He kissed her cheek softly, as though she had been a child, then held the door open for her to pass through.

Lucy went, her heart heavy with guilt and misery.

'That particular exercise seems not to have advanced us any

further,' said Justin. 'Did you gain the impression that your man was holding anything back?'

'Difficult to say, sir. Indignant in a restrained way, of course, at being subjected to more questioning, but that might be a cover for something else,' replied Watts judicially. 'Y'know, sir, attack's the best method of defence. Could be nothing in it, though.'

Justin nodded. 'And Peyton? Anything there?'

'Deep one, I reckon. Don't miss much and gives as little away as his master. I took it on myself to hang about a bit after I left the house and saw Cleveland come out shortly afterwards. I followed him, though I'd to be quick getting a hackney. He fetched up eventually at a lawyer's in Lincoln's Inn Fields. Brass plate on the door – Binns & Moody. Wondered if I should go in and make inquiries about what our man wanted there but decided against it. Thought I'd consult you first, sir.'

'Hm. Tricky. Quite natural for a man to consult his lawyer from time to time. He might have been seeking advice over discouraging persecution from Bow Street, who knows?' suggested Justin with a chuckle. 'Anyway, it's inadvisable to make a stir there, I think. Did he stay long?'

'Not more than ten minutes. Only thing is, sir, he left his curricle at the Cock in Fleet Street and walked through to the Fields by way of *Chancery Lane*.'

Watts paused significantly.

'Hm. Might mean anything or nothing. It was a fine morning and a man like Cleveland don't get much exercise when the House is sitting. All the same, Joe, since I've nothing pressing for you to undertake at present, why not make discreet inquiries about this lawyer? You may turn up something, and we've not much to go on so far. Discreet is the watchword, mind. We don't want to scare our bird off, whoever he may be.'

'Never fear, sir. I'll see if I can find one of the clerks in a nearby tavern. A free pint of ale makes 'em open their mouths in more senses than one. What of the doctor, sir – anything there?'

Justin considered. 'No, although I gained a strong impression that he knew something. Whether it would have helped us or not,' – he shrugged – 'I couldn't say. He's a shrewd man. Moreover he's in a stronger position to discover the secrets of others than the defunct Yarnton, or even – and this is a bold word! – the indomitable Runners themselves.'

'Maybe.' Watts sounded unimpressed. 'All the same, sir, I'll back you to bring home the bacon.'

The Velmonds' first dinner party was a modest affair with only ten people present including the hosts. Nevertheless, Lucilla made it the occasion of anxious consultations with her cook and housekeeper, somewhat to the amusement of those worthies, who were quite competent to produce a creditable repast without milady troubling herself in the matter. She had so endeared herself already to her staff, however, that they took no offence and indulgently allowed her to think her suggestions had been invaluable.

She was acquainted with all her guests, some more than others. The Honourable Giles Aylesford and his pretty, if rather plump, wife had called upon Velmond and herself in the customary manner soon after their marriage. Mr Aylesford, like Mr Bradfield, was one of her husband's close associates. As for Viscount and Lady Rutherford, Mr Rutherford, kind Lady Quainton and dear Anthea, they produced none of the shrinking feelings which so often assailed her in the company of strangers.

'Is Mrs Bradfield to come up to Town at some time during the season?' Lady Quainton asked Bradfield, who was sitting at table between herself and Lucy.

'She may possibly come for a day or two next week, ma'am,' he replied. 'That is, if she can tear herself away from the children – and the country, which she much prefers to Town.'

'For my part I cannot abide more than a week or so in the country,' said Mrs Aylesford with a light laugh. 'It is vastly more melancholy than London when the weather is bad – all those muddy lanes and dripping hedgerows! Besides, one can be so isolated, dependent on neighbours who often live miles distant.'

'We're fortunate in having several families quite close, ma'am, with whom we're on excellent terms. The Wingraves, whose property adjoins ours, are particular friends and I dare say scarce a day passes when my wife and Lady Wingrave do not meet.'

'How very pleasant! I don't recall ever meeting Lady Wingrave, though of course I know that she's Lady Kinver's daughter,' said Mrs Aylesford.

'She, too, prefers the country,' put in Lady Quainton, 'though occasionally she visits her mama here to do some shopping. But it is all a matter of what one becomes accustomed to, for I can recall a time before her marriage when Maria Wingrave was all agog for balls and parties. That was six years ago, of course. Now she's a matron with three young children, I dare say she sets less store by such frivolities.'

'The sobering influence of matrimony,' said Anthea with a twinkle.

'I doubt matrimony will sober you greatly, puss,' remarked her father, with mock severity.

Justin shot a quizzical glance at her and the conversation drifted into other channels.

Later, when the gentlemen were sitting alone over their wine, mention was made of the murder.

'Curious business,' remarked Aylesford. 'I wonder if it will ever be solved? I can't think that anyone would take Yarnton seriously enough to kill him. He'd been making malicious remarks for long enough, God knows. Some found them devilish amusing too.'

'Others found them damnably offensive,' said Velmond shortly.

'Oh, quite.' For a moment Aylesford had forgotten Velmond's quarrel with the dead man. He had not been present at the soirée himself, so had heard the story at second hand. 'Bad taste, of course.'

'I believe you've taken some interest in the affair,' remarked Bradfield to Justin. 'Have you turned up anything yet to give you a scent?'

Justin shrugged. 'Afraid not. Yarnton made some cryptic remarks concerning a certain Mr Thompson which I felt might possibly be relevant, but those who heard appear not to find any significance in them.'

Bradfield laughed. 'Oh, yes, I recall his saying that – it afforded me some quiet amusement at the time.'

The others stared at him.

'Amusement?' Justin asked sharply.

'Why, yes. You see, I do happen to know someone of that name, quite unconnected with Yarnton's man, of course, if there ever was such a fellow, and it wasn't just one of his take-ins.'

'Who's the man you know?' demanded Velmond.

'My land agent in Sussex, that's what made it so deuced ludicrous,' replied Bradfield with a chuckle. 'A most respectable man, nearing sixty, and a highly unlikely target for Yarnton's scandalmongering. Now can you see why I found the reference amusing?'

They agreed that this might be so and the conversation moved on to other topics.

Chapter X

Lady Quainton had been intending for some time to carry out her promise to Justin that she would question Lady Kinver about the name Thompson, but no suitable opportunity had presented itself. At the Velmonds' dinner party Justin gave her a gentle reminder, so she set off for her friend's house in Curzon Street on the following afternoon.

She found Lady Kinver sitting alone over the fire in a small parlour at the back of the house. She was evidently in low spirits, for she could barely summon up a smile when her friend was shown into the room.

'I trust my visit isn't inconvenient, Jane?' said Lady Quainton, kissing the other's cold cheek. 'I only looked in to see how you did, but I can easily come at another time.'

Jane Kinver made an attempt to rouse herself. 'No, not at all, Cassie. Pray remove your bonnet and pelisse and make yourself comfortable. Would you care for some tea?'

Reflecting that Jane was evidently a trifle strung up and that a cup of tea was the panacea for all ills, Lady Quainton accepted this offer.

The tea was served and Lady Kinver stretched out an unsteady hand to the teapot, then drew it back.

'Would you mind doing the office for me, Cassie? I don't seem able to manage.'

'My dear Jane, whatever is wrong?' asked her friend in some concern. 'Are you ill? I've thought lately that you looked a trifle peaky.'

'Dr Wetherby has just left me,' admitted Jane Kinver. 'He's been attending me ever since that – that dreadful affair at Maria Windlesham's! He says it's simply an affliction of the nerves, but I don't seem able –' her voice broke – 'to pull myself together! I keep going over everything in my mind and wondering where it will all lead – dear God, I don't know what to do!'

'First of all you're going to drink a good, strong cup of tea,' said Lady Quainton firmly, pouring out two cups and setting one before her hostess. 'And then you may tell me all about your trouble. No – not a word until you've had this.'

Jane Kinver summoned up a weak smile.

'You were always the practical one, Cassie,' she said, but she obediently sipped the tea.

There was silence in the room for several minutes, then Jane set down her cup.

'If only that odious man hadn't been murdered!' she burst out. 'I've never known an easy moment since then, dreading that everything would come out!'

Cassandra Quainton wisely said nothing, waiting for what was to follow.

'All these years I've prayed that I'd be able to suppress it! He'd discovered something, that was plain by what he said, but I dare say he would never have gone beyond hints and sly allusions – you know his way! But, of course, when he was murdered it meant that Bow Street would be investigating and secrets would come to light – and not only Bow Street, for I've heard rumours that the youngest Rutherford has been asking questions, particularly it seems, about – about the remarks Yarnton made to some of us concerning Mr Thompson!' Jane Kinver went on in an explosive fashion. 'And when they *do* find out about *him* – '

'Jane,' interrupted Lady Quainton imperatively, 'are you trying to tell me that *you* have anything to do with this mysterious Thompson? That in fact you know who he is?'

'Not who he is but *what*! Yes, that I do know!'

There had been no opportunity at the Velmonds' dinner party for Justin to acquaint his godmother with what he had learned of Thompson's activities, so she had no inkling of where this conversation was leading. Overcome with curiosity, yet slightly ashamed of this in view of her friend's distress, she could not wait to hear the rest.

'*What he is*?' she repeated. 'I don't at all comprehend your meaning. Pray explain, my dear.'

'He's an extortionist – a blackmailer!'

Cassandra Quainton gasped incredulously.

'I've been paying him blackmail for the past five years! The sum amounts to almost twenty thousand pounds by now! And I can see no end to it – I must go on paying!'

'Good God!'

It was an unusually forceful expletive for the gentle Lady Quainton, but nothing less could do justice to her feelings of outrage and amazement.

For some time both ladies were silent, Jane Kinver cowering in her chair with a hopeless expression. Presently Lady Quainton pulled herself together.

'But blackmail – *you*, Jane?' she asked in an incredulous tone. 'I cannot credit it! Surely there can be nothing whatever in your life to justify extortion? Unless – '

She paused. How well did one know one's friends after all, even the most intimate of them? There might have been some episode. . . .

'My dear,' she continued gently, 'perhaps there was something you kept secret even from me? Some love affair that would have created a monstrous scandal if it ever became known?'

Jane Kinver shook her head. 'No. I did have a secret, Cassie, but it was not mine. There was never any man in my life after I wed Charles. My secret concerned my poor girl, Maria, and somehow this devil Thompson found it out.'

'Maria,' repeated the other thoughtfully.

'Yes, I'll tell you of it now, dearest Cassie, though all these years I've kept it from everyone, even Charles. Most of all Charles, for as you know, he was in failing health for some time before he died in the August of 1811. Indeed, the fear that it might come to his ears by accident was a constant nightmare to me.'

She stopped, the tears standing in her eyes. Lady Quainton placed a hand over hers in sympathy but said nothing. What was there to say in the face of such suffering?

'You recall how Maria was, at seventeen years of age,' continued Jane Kinver presently. 'A trifle giddy perhaps, full of fun and gig, thoughtless of consequences like most young girls. Charles was ill and the doctors advised a stay in Bath to take the waters. Maria said Bath was too stuffy and she wouldn't go

86

with us. I couldn't possibly leave her here in Town with only the servants to look after her so I packed her off to my sister Olivia Hardwick in a village in Buckinghamshire. I thought she'd be safe enough there, but I hadn't reckoned with Maria being able to twist her aunt around her thumb. She was allowed to do anything she wanted it seemed, and there were several young men in that neighbourhood, some eligible, some not. She flirted outrageously with all of them, as we discovered afterwards, in particular a young army captain named Tilsworth, who was on leave at the time.'

She broke off again in distress and it was some moments before she could continue.

'I don't know how to tell you the rest, Cassie – it's too shameful! And Maria our only child. She was to have her come-out in the following season and we had such hopes for her happiness! But there, I mustn't indulge in self-pity, and in the end, things turned out better than might have been expected. I dare say you can hazard a guess as to what kind of fix she got herself into. She became pregnant.'

Lady Quainton had by now anticipated this outcome but, nevertheless, she drew in a quick breath.

'I didn't know – she never told me. She returned home in September at the same time as ourselves and she knew how matters stood about the middle of October as I discovered later. But she kept her secret until the end of November, when mercifully she had a miscarriage. Then, of course, I had to know. I won't dwell on my feelings, Cassie, but you may well understand that my chief anxiety was to keep it from my husband in his precarious state of health. I shall never know how I managed that but thank God he suspected nothing. No one else was in the secret but the doctor and Maria's old nanny, who was still with us at that time.'

'My poor Jane! But why did not Maria marry the father of her child? She must surely have written to inform him of her condition?'

'No, for she kept hoping and hoping that matters would right themselves, and by the time she was forced to accept the situation it was too late. The man was Captain Tilsworth. He'd been recalled to the Peninsula shortly after Maria left my sister's house and in a few weeks he was killed in action. My sister sent us the news in October but even then Maria said nothing. It was some days after her miscarriage before she would tell me who was responsible. At first she refused again and again, ask as I might.'

'As you say,' said Lady Quainton thoughtfully, 'although it was a dreadful business, it might have turned out a deal worse. I recall that Maria did have her come-out in the season preceding your husband's death and she married Sir Rupert Wingrave in July of that year. You must have felt profoundly relieved to see her safely settled.'

'Indeed I was. Naturally I had to keep to my original plan to bring her out that season, for fear her father, or others, might wonder if I did not. When Wingrave offered for her so soon after her come-out I could only hope and pray that the marriage would prove a success. But so it has, Cassie – you know she has three little ones in the nursery and seems quite content. Thank Heaven for it.'

Lady Quainton nodded. 'Yes indeed. But tell me, Jane, when did the blackmailing begin?'

'A few months after Charles died when Maria had been about three months married. I shall never forget my horror on receiving that first letter! The writer knew all about Maria's – indiscretion – before marriage, and threatened to go to Wingrave with the story unless I paid the sum of two thousand pounds! I was instructed to direct a packet containing the money to a Mr Thompson and forward it to the receiving office at St Albans. Imagine how I felt, Cassie!'

'It was indeed a terrible dilemma, my poor Jane! I suppose you felt you dared not risk showing the letter to anyone who might have advised you? Your lawyer, for instance?'

'Oh, no, how could I? There was not much time, moreover – this fiend gave a date by which the packet must arrive. But in any event I wouldn't risk my only child's happiness for the sake of a paltry two thousand pounds. I am not exactly purse-pinched, my dear, as you well know. Of course,' she added glumly, 'I didn't know then that the demand would be repeated every six months until I should have parted with a considerable sum. Even so, I still think it better to buy this creature's silence than to risk Maria's undoing. Would not you in a like predicament?'

'Very possibly, though as I have no family it's difficult to say. Tell me, though, did you always have to send the money to the same receiving office – I think you said St Albans?'

'No. It was to a different one on each occasion. I don't recollect, precisely – Barnet, I think, Reading, Watford, some in London – oh, I've been paying out for so many years now I cannot recall all the places specified! Not that it can possibly signify!'

'It might,' demurred her friend thoughtfully. 'I suppose you have no notion who this blackmailer could be?'

Jane Kinver shook her head.

'No, for there were so few people in the secret and I knew I could rely utterly on their discretion.'

'In such cases, of course, something often leaks out quite inadvertently. One has only to consider the occasions when we ourselves have perhaps let something drop which we would have cut out our tongues rather than reveal – a hint would have been enough to an unscrupulous villain such as this man must be. He would follow it up relentlessly until he'd uncovered the whole. Does no such possibility occur to you?'

'Only if Maria had confided her secret to someone other than myself, and that she swore she did *not* do! Poor child, she told me later that she was scared out of her wits when she discovered her condition and kept hoping all would come right so that no one need ever know. And later, when it came to the miscarriage, all was managed with the utmost discretion. I was fortunately in the house at the time and nanny was already with her in her bedchamber.'

'I suppose it isn't possible that Captain Tilsworth should have revealed the, er, nature of his relationship with Maria to a third party?' persisted Lady Quainton.

'Why on earth should he do such an abominable thing? After all he was an officer and a gentleman and it would be in his own interest to keep silent about the affair. But all this is beside the point, Cassie. Knowing the identity of the blackmailer can avail me nothing – any attempt to bring this monster to book can only result in the scandal becoming known! That's what so terrifies me about the inquiries into Yarnton's murder. I could not bear it if after all I have suffered these years, Maria's secret should come to light!'

She broke down on these words and Lady Quainton comforted her until she had regained some degree of tranquillity.

'But you know,' Lady Quainton said gently at last, 'it will not do, Jane. How long will you go on meeting these demands and robbing your daughter of her inheritance? No, don't answer me for a moment, but consider another question I am about to put to you. If it were possible to discover this blackmailer without revealing Maria's secret to any save only one person – '

'No!' cried Jane Kinver vehemently. 'I'll not believe that possible – I dare not take such a risk!'

'Yet you have already realized that Bow Street may discover your secret in the course of their inquiries. Before the authorities proceed so far, would it not be preferable to entrust it to a private individual, one of your own social order who would find the means to keep it quiet? I think perhaps you know to whom I refer?'

Lady Kinver nodded. 'Your godson, Justin Rutherford. I know he's been asking questions, though I'm not sure why. But, but, oh, I don't at all know, Cassie!'

'Justin seeks to clear Velmond of all suspicion by discovering the murderer for himself. Moreover, by what he told me, he has the blessing of the chief magistrate at Bow Street, so doubtless he could bring strong influence to bear in that quarter on your behalf. He asked me for an account of Yarnton's remarks at that fateful soirée and seemed vastly intrigued by the reference to Mr Thompson. He would be yet more intrigued could he know what you've just told me! Truly, Jane, cannot you see that your wisest course would be to confide the whole to him? Should you not care to discuss so intimate a subject with a young unmarried man, I will readily engage to act for you.'

For some time Lady Kinver continued to protest that she could not, but eventually her friend managed to persuade her.

Chapter XI

On most evenings Mr Dick Probert, senior clerk to the lawyers Binns & Moody in Lincoln's Inn Fields, took a tankard of ale at a nearby tavern before returning to his modest home in Carey Street. While at his place of business he was efficient and self-contained with little to say beyond what was necessary to the junior clerks under him; but once in the cosy atmosphere of the Wheatsheaf he allowed himself to relax. The truth was that he was a lonely man and therefore ready to engage in casual conversation with any respectable, solitary drinker like himself, though he always avoided the noisier groups.

Joe Watts, strolling into the tavern on the evening of his consultation with Justin Rutherford, summed his man up at a glance. He carried his tankard over to the settle which Probert was occupying alone.

'Mind if I sit here?' he asked carelessly.

'Not at all, pray do,' replied Probert, striking a careful balance between politeness and a more positive welcome.

He eyed the newcomer warily as he spoke, trying to assess his place in the scheme of things. A tradesman, perhaps, in a thriving way of business? He had the air of one accustomed to controlling staff. Not, he thought, a clerk; he lacked the pallid complexion of the indoor, sedentary man.

He permitted himself to chat to Watts on a number of innocuous topics, sat there for his accustomed time – less than an hour – and departed with a civil goodnight.

Watts came into the Wheatsheaf on the following evening and again sat by his quarry. This time the conversation grew more personal, especially after Watts had insisted on buying Probert another drink.

'I never do take another, Mr Rowlands,' protested Probert

half-heartedly. 'But seeing as I'm enjoying your company and you're so kind as to offer, I'll make an exception. I've not much to go home to, and that's the truth, since my dear wife died.'

Watts made the appropriate remarks of commiseration and asked when the melancholy event had taken place.

'Three years since,' replied the clerk in sombre tones. 'And me left with a fifteen-year-old girl to bring up on my own, barring a little help from my sister who lives nearby. But she and Kitty don't get on, no use saying they do, so she don't come in often these days. Have you any family, Mr Rowlands?'

'Neither child nor wife,' said Watts cheerfully. 'Reckon I get along better that way. Suits me, any road.'

'There's much in what you say,' agreed the other. 'I don't mind admitting that my daughter's a constant source of anxiety to me. She's in the house all day on her own and dear knows what she gets up to when my back's turned. She's past eighteen now.'

Watts nodded sympathetically. 'Often frisky at that age, young ladies,' he ventured.

'You may certainly say so, Mr Rowlands. I used to like her to look in on me occasionally at the office during our midday break but I had to put a stop to it.' He looked grave and clicked his tongue. 'What with the juniors casting sheep's eyes at her, for she's not a bad-looking girl, even though I've a father's natural partiality – '

Watts indicated that he was sure the young lady could fully substantiate her father's claims.

'Yes, well, I could keep *them* in order, right enough,' continued Probert. 'But when it came to another young fellow – secretary of one of our clients – I felt it safer to tell her not to come any more. He wouldn't mean right by her, not a man in his position, I'll be bound.'

'Would that young fellow's name chance to be Peyton?' asked Watts casually. 'Secretary to Mr Henry Cleveland, Member of Parliament?'

Probert looked a trifle disturbed and hesitated.

'Why, yes,' he admitted reluctantly. 'Though I ought not to divulge the names of our clients. This young Peyton sometimes comes on errands from his employer, not on his own behalf. Do you know him?'

Watts nodded. 'I have some business dealings with Mr Cleveland's household, you see. Between ourselves,' – he adopted a confidential tone – 'I don't find that party a good payer, not by any means.'

Probert pursed his lips. 'You mean Mr Cleveland? That don't surprise me by what our Mr Binns lets drop from time to time.'

The unaccustomed extra pint of ale had made Probert more than usually expansive, but now he was suddenly overcome by the feeling that he had been indiscreet. He drained his tankard, bade his new-found friend a hurried goodnight and departed.

'I thought it might be that,' said Justin looking satisfied.

'Did you indeed, you wretched boy?' demanded Lady Quainton, smiling in spite of herself. 'Upon my word, you terrify me at times! Are no secrets safe from your prying mind, I wonder?'

She had just finished recounting to him the story told her by Lady Kinver.

'It wasn't really so very difficult to guess, after all, godmama, I already knew there was a blackmailer at work, as I've just explained to you. Therefore it seemed a reasonable assumption that Lady Kinver's distress at that soirée would indicate that she was yet another victim. I couldn't cast her in the role of murderer, so what remained?'

'No, indeed, I should think not! But I do feel sincerely sorry for poor little Lucy Velmond. I knew she could never be keeping an assignation with some man in Petticoat Lane, but I never dreamt what the monstrous truth would be! Whatever can that innocent child have done to give this villain a hold upon her? Not that I mean to press you for details,' she added hastily.

'Just as well, for I don't possess 'em,' replied Justin lightly. 'It's the lady's secret until she chooses to divulge it to Velmond, which I urged her to do with all possible speed.'

'And has she done so?'

'I don't know – I must inquire of Anthea. But to return to the present case, ma'am, although you seem to have asked most of the pertinent questions, there are one or two points that occur to me. In particular, I would like to interview the family nurse, if that could be arranged. Knowing Lady Kinver's daughter intimately from childhood she may be able to shed more light on the affair.'

'Yet it seems clear enough,' demurred Lady Quainton.

'Yes, but one can never tell. A first-hand account often reveals some important fact that is lost in a report from a third party. Only consider how invaluable I've found your eye-witness account of the events on the night of Yarnton's murder, for example.'

She laughed. 'Now you are trying to turn me up sweet. But I'll speak to Jane Kinver and see if that can be arranged for you.'

Accordingly Justin was seated a few days later in the neat parlour of a small cottage situated on Paddington Green.

Mrs Barton, one-time nurse to Maria, was a small woman with a pleasant, somewhat wrinkled face and greying hair tidily arranged beneath a snowy white cap. She had been prepared by Lady Kinver for this visit and accepted it quite calmly, willing to assist the Honourable Justin Rutherford if possible.

'I would like you to consider, Mrs Barton,' he began, after some civil preliminaries, 'whether it's at all possible that anyone else in Lady Kinver's household should have learned of this affair. Some of the servants, perhaps?'

'No, sir. There were no servants in that part of the house at the time, it being early afternoon. Miss Maria had gone to lie down with the headache, as she said, and I looked in to see how she did. I soon realized there was more than the headache and fetched my lady from her boudoir on the same floor. Fortunately the doctor was in the house paying a call on the master, who was always in indifferent health. There was no stir made in bringing him to Miss Maria – it was but a few steps along the landing with none of the staff by to see or hear aught.'

'And you're confident that no word was dropped – accidentally, of course – afterwards, to give rise to talk among the servants?'

She bridled a little. 'Who would let fall anything do you

94

suppose, sir? Not my lady and certainly not myself! I've never mentioned it to this day.'

'Of course not,' he said soothingly. 'And a doctor's discretion is naturally to be relied upon. Who was the medico, by the way?'

'Why, Dr Wetherby of course. My lady would have none but the best doctor to attend the master and Miss Maria.'

'I see.'

He frowned thoughtfully and fell silent for a while. Nanny Barton studied him meanwhile, liking what she saw. The alert brown eyes showed intelligence, the firm chin decision, and the mobile mouth a sense of humour. She had watched too many children grow up not to be able to interpret such physical signs. Here was a gentleman to be trusted with a secret of some delicacy, of that she was sure; though it seemed an eccentric thing that he should interest himself in such dubious matters. She wished there was some way in which she could help him to find the villain who had been extorting money from her ladyship for so many years, a fact which had appalled her when Lady Kinver had revealed it only yesterday. But there was nothing she could think of, nothing at all. Unless. . .

'Let us consider another aspect of the case,' resumed Justin. 'My own family nurse knew all of us better than our parents and I dare say the same is true of yourself and Lady Kinver's daughter?'

Nanny Barton smiled. 'Well, I'll not deny that I was up to most of Miss Maria's tricks, when she was a child at any rate. I can't speak for when she came out of the schoolroom, for young ladies are another matter you know, sir.'

'Do I not?' he said feelingly, thinking of his niece Anthea. 'But it does occur to me that you may be in a better position than Lady Kinver to say whether or not your erstwhile charge may have confided her predicament to any other person than her mother.'

She considered this for a moment with furrowed brows.

'No, I don't think it for a moment, sir,' she said presently in a decided tone. 'Had she confided in anyone it would have been me. She knew she could always rely on me, come what may. But

95

she was too frightened, poor lamb, and too inexperienced to be certain. She waited, hoping and trusting all would come right, and so told no one at all of her plight. There was one thing, though . . . I don't know, it might not signify – '

'Tell me.' He leaned forward eagerly.

'Why, there'd been a lady visitor sitting with the two of them – my lady and Miss Maria – when Miss Maria excused herself saying she had the headache. And she's a vastly sharp lady, too, that Mrs Cleveland, not one to miss much. It's just possible she might have suspected something – I wonder now.'

'Mrs Cleveland,' repeated Justin pensively. 'Well, I fear this is unfamiliar territory to me, Mrs Barton. You must be the better judge of what likelihood there was of any suspicion being aroused. Personally I would think it remote.'

'Ah, but a nod's as good as a wink to a blind horse,' said nanny, reverting to the axioms with which she had puzzled her charges in childhood.

Justin grinned. 'I recall my nurse trying out that one on me. I'm not sure even now what she meant.'

Mrs Barton smiled in return. 'I dare say she meant, sir, that it's best to keep a still tongue in your head and your eyes fully opened.'

'I'd certainly agree with that. One more thing, with your indulgence, Mrs Barton, and then I have done. Do you know what female friends Lady Kinver's daughter would have in her aunt's neighbourhood in Buckinghamshire, where I collect she was staying for a month or so while her parents were in Bath?'

She shook her head. 'There I can't help you, sir, for if there were any, they must have been new acquaintances. She'd never stayed before alone with Mrs Hardwick, just going with her parents for short visits once or twice a year. And as Mrs Hardwick has no family of her own, other children never came to the house.'

'Disappointing,' he admitted with a rueful look. 'I had hoped – '

'I think I know, sir,' she interrupted, her gaze sharpening. 'You're thinking that a friend of Miss Maria's might have got wind of how she was carrying on and let it slip to someone so's it reached this villain who's been blackmailing my poor lady.

And so it could have been, I'll not deny.'

'Almost anyone could have chanced to acquire the information, of course, but a female friend seems more likely. Did this Captain Tilsworth have sisters, do you know?'

'No, he did not. But,' – reluctantly – 'I do have some doubts, sir, I must admit.'

'Doubts?'

'Yes. About Captain Tilsworth.'

He waited for her to overcome an evident reluctance to say more. At last she made up her mind.

'Dead men tell no tales, Mr Rutherford. And Miss Maria could be – devious – at times. With so much at stake, and perhaps wanting to protect someone else – well, suppose she wasn't telling the truth when she blamed the captain?'

Chapter XII

*W*e caught that other bully lad,'
reported Watts. 'Nothing out of him but a lot of tarrididdle, like
his mate. Said they were hired to keep a watch on Yarnton's
place, but they reckon they can't say who by, seeing as Sims
fixed it with them on t'other's behalf. And no luck yet in finding
that same cove from the description given by Sims, if you can
rightly call it a description.'

'I didn't have any strong expectations in that quarter, I must
say. What news from Binns & Moody's clerk?'

'Not much there either, sir. One thing, though, I'd over-
looked. I called in at Bow Street to check it. Binns & Moody
was Yarnton's lawyer too. Don't know if it signifies that he and
the MP used the same firm?'

Justin pondered this for a few moments. 'Any connection
between our principals can be significant but I must admit
that at present I fail to see where it fits. We'll file it away for
future reference. Did you discover anything else?'

Watts shook his head. 'That man Probert, their senior clerk,
was a sight too discreet for my purpose, though I tried to wet his
tongue so's it would wag. He confirmed by a hint that Cleveland's in deep water but we pretty well knew that already. He
grumbled a lot of the time about his young daughter – seems
he's a widower and she's a flighty piece. He said he had to stop
her from coming to see him at the office on account of his junior
clerks making up to her. Not only them, either, it seems, but
that young fellow Peyton, Cleveland's secretary, who
sometimes goes there on his employer's business.'

Justin grinned. 'The first personal information we've so far
collected about Peyton. Again, it's not significant as far as we
can tell. Doubtless he does have an eye for the petticoats, like
most men of his age – odd if he didn't. His social position's a

trifle ambivalent. One wonders how he passes his leisure time and what friends he has. Obviously he don't mix in Cleveland's set. Perhaps we should look into all that presently. Meanwhile, however, I've some news for you of the utmost importance.'

He recounted briefly all he had learned of Lady Kinver's dealings with Thompson, finishing by going over the interview with Nurse Barton. At the conclusion Watts emitted a low, prolonged whistle.

'You always did think there might be other victims, sir. Gawd, though, twenty thousand pounds! And been going on for five years! No wonder this Thompson murdered Yarnton.'

'The devil of it is, we don't seem much closer to tracking the fellow down,' said Justin ruefully. 'I'd give much to know, Joe, what that notebook of Yarnton's contained, but we may depend that it's been destroyed by now. He'd be a fool to keep it and I'd lay any odds he's far from that. Suppose we examine the facts we do possess.'

He paused, collecting his thoughts.

'From what we know at present, two of our suspects definitely had access to the secrets used for extortion, namely, Cleveland and Wetherby. Unfortunately we can't be certain that either of them knew *both* secrets. Take Cleveland first. His daughter was at school with Lady Velmond and learned of her misdemeanour. The girl would certainly have talked of it at home as schoolgirls are incurable chatterboxes. Assuming Cleveland to be Thompson, he would have stored the information away against a time when it might be useful, namely when the penniless schoolgirl Lucy has become a wealthy man's wife. His possession of Lady Kinver's secret is less certain, however, depending as it does solely on an impression gained by Nurse Barton.'

'We do know that he's under the hatches, sir, don't we? And also that he's probably been involved in dubious dealings on the Stock Exchange. He needs the money, which makes him a likely candidate.'

'True. I'd like firm evidence that he did know of the Kinver affair though. How to get it?'

'Lady Quainton might help there, sir. Talk to Mrs Cleveland, worm it out of her the way females do.'

Justin frowned. 'There's something vastly distasteful about using a wife to incriminate her husband.'

'They're only too pleased to do it most times in my line of business. May be different with the Quality, of course.'

His tone indicated doubt.

'Not sure that it is,' replied Justin, confirming this cynical view. 'We could perhaps try it. But Mrs Cleveland's away from home at present, visiting her daughter.'

'There's another way, sir. I've been cultivating the acquaintance of one of the housemaids there – thought she might come in useful as a source of information.'

Justin chuckled. 'Oh you have, have you? Pretty, is she?'

Watts winked. 'Not bad, sir, very well to pass, as you might say.'

'It's always agreeable to be able to combine business with pleasure. All the same I don't see that this young female could provide the answers we need at present, although she may prove useful for keeping an eye on the household in general. You have my full permission to continue the association, Joe, though I trust you'll have a care not to get yourself into Parson's Mousetrap,' he finished with a grin.

'Gawd, no,' said Watts fervently. 'I never go that far, guv'nor!'

'To return to our sheep, as the French say. Let's consider the good doctor. He has full knowledge of the Kinver secret, of course, but could he have discovered Lady Velmond's?'

'He's been attending the lady,' pointed out Watts. 'She might have let something out to him.'

'But only since she received the blackmail letter, recollect. Before that she had no nervous symptoms and therefore no need of his services.'

'True, I forgot. Well, he might have been chatting to Mrs Cleveland or even her married daughter, when she lived at home with her parents.'

'Now we're back at speculation. Moreover, even if either of our suspects had been in possession of the full facts and we could prove that to our satisfaction, we'd still need more tangible evidence to convict this so-called Thompson of murder. Another demand for blackmail might help us to track him down.'

Watts pursed his lips.

'Should think he'd lie low at present, sir, wouldn't you?'

Justin considered this. 'No, why should he do so? He's no reason to suppose that anyone other than the victims – and, of course, the unfortunate Yarnton – knows anything of his blackmailing activities.'

'We've been asking questions about Thompson, though.'

'True, but in such a way that we sounded completely in the dark ourselves. Moreover, there's nothing whatever to cause him to suspect that either of his victims has confided in a third party. Lady Kinver hasn't done so in five years, so why should she start now? As for Lady Velmond, it must be plain to the meanest intelligence that the poor little creature is easily scared and unlikely to do anything to put her marriage in jeopardy. Not that I consider it at all likely that she'll receive a second demand for some time. Our man is by far too canny to overplay his hand and will realize that the ready is hard to come by in that quarter.'

Watts nodded.

'I think it probable, though,' continued Justin, 'that Lady Kinver may be approached again before long. She's been receiving demands at regular six-monthly intervals over the past five years and the last of these arrived in October. They come in the first week of the month, so I'm informed. No doubt you've noticed that we've just embarked on April? That should indicate that one may arrive any day.'

'B' God, sir, if he does send a demand to the lady, we should be able to grab him, right enough! That's to say if he follows the same method as for t'other lady, and names a particular office and a date for payment.'

Justin nodded. 'I'm told that's been the way of it over past years and there's no reason to suppose he'll vary it this time. Of course there's no means of telling exactly when he'll collect. We made inquiries at the receiving office ten days after the date given to Lady Velmond and no one could inform us precisely when that packet was collected, much less by whom. It may mean mounting a close watch at the receiving office for several days, even weeks. He'll collect at his convenience, early or late, according, perhaps, to the state of his pockets, what?'

'Well, we can always put another Runner on to it, sir, besides myself.'

'True. In the meantime I'd like to know more about both Cleveland and Wetherby, as at present they're the favourites in the field. I fear we may need to seek information by less, ah, legitimate methods than we've employed so far. An examination of their private papers would be helpful. That being so, you may possibly wish to disassociate yourself from my activities? As an officer of the law, I mean.'

'No fear, sir. That pretty housemaid will come in handy for getting me into Cleveland's place.'

'Then I'll take the doctor. We may perhaps both meet in gaol, Watts, eh?'

Justin and his niece were dancing together at Lady Rutherford's first ball of the season, an event which her brother-in-law had felt obliged to attend. They made a handsome pair and more than one wistful or envious glance was sent in their direction. The young ladies sighed over the dark-haired gentleman with a humorous twist to his mouth, who looked so distinguished in his black coat, pantaloons and intricately tied cravat. The gentlemen found it difficult to take their eyes off his delightful partner, a bewitching figure in soft pink gauze over silk, her hair dressed with a topknot of ringlets bound in a circlet of artificial pink rosebuds.

At the moment she was pouting, an expression which only made her elfin features more attractive.

'You've treated me in a monstrous shabby fashion,' she complained. 'You promised to keep me informed of everything you've discovered, and here am I, no wiser, though you must have discovered something by now, needle-witted as you are! And don't suppose I haven't noticed that you've been avoiding me lately – anyone might suppose I'd contracted the plague!'

'Doing it too brown, fair child,' he said lightly. 'Anyone so mistaken as to entertain such a suspicion must wonder at the numbers of men present this evening who are evidently ready and eager to run the risk of infection. Only look about you –

Grassington, for instance, is positively goggle-eyed!'

She could not help following the direction of his gaze, then turned back quickly and laughed.

'His eyes do tend to resemble a frog's at the best of times,' she whispered. 'But what have you to say for yourself, you wretch? Don't think I'm not aware that you're trying to turn the subject!'

'No, indeed. We are both too knacky by half to hope to deceive each other. Well, there are things I will tell you presently, when we can be assured of privacy, but certainly not on the ballroom floor. Tell me, who is the lady dancing with Velmond?'

'Oh, that's Mrs Bradfield,' she replied, having glanced at the couple in question. 'She arrived in Town only a few days ago, but of course mama included her in the invitation, as she'd already asked Mr Bradfield.'

'Have you any previous acquaintance with her?' he asked.

'No, for she's a little older than I and was out while I was still in the schoolroom. Why, do you want me to assist in another of your seductions?'

She accompanied this remark with a saucy look which made several gentlemen nearby decide that Rutherford must be cut out ruthlessly for the next dance, even if the fellow was most respectably related to their divinity.

He sighed. 'I regret to inform you that my seductions have not been prospering of late, with or without your assistance.'

'That is quite your own fault. Any number of my friends have been angling shamelessly for an introduction to you.'

'Alas, my dear, I am sorry to tell you that matrimony is not my present aim, while I'm quite sure your friends have decidedly opposite views.'

'Well, yes, I dare say you are right,' she conceded. 'And I must admit that I myself find matrimony a lowering prospect, in spite of all mama's encouragement to fix my interest with some one of the undoubtedly pleasant and eligible gentlemen who seem willing to take the risk of having me for a wife. There is so much one wants to do before settling into a life of domesticity!'

'What would you like to do?' he asked, amused.

'Travel,' she answered promptly. 'Not only France, where everyone goes since the peace, but Italy, Greece, Turkey – like Lady Mary Wortley Montagu, you know.'

'And perhaps, like her, discover something as useful as inoculation against the smallpox?' he quizzed her. 'Though you must forgive me for pointing out that it was a mere male – Dr Jenner – who improved upon the original discovery.'

'But that was several years later,' she objected. 'Besides, is it not the way of the world? Only the male sex ever really find the opportunity for serious study.'

He regarded her with respect. 'A bluestocking, eh? Well, perhaps you may live to see changes, my dear. Meanwhile, stick to your guns and don't allow either your mama or the usages of society to chivvy you into marriage before you're ready. But don't tell her I said so, for pity's sake!'

True to his word he did confide to her his latest information during a brief private interlude after supper and before the dancing recommenced. He told her everything except the precise details of Maria Kinver's indiscretion, which she was at liberty to guess at for herself.

She looked reflective.

'Do you not find it interesting that the nurse thought she was lying? But I expect you'll look into that. I can certainly be useful to you, Justin, in finding out from Lucy if she ever confided her trouble to Dr Wetherby. She seems to be enjoying herself tolerably well this evening, but would you believe, she still hasn't told Velmond the truth? Mind you, I don't altogether blame her,' she added, fair-mindedly, 'for matters fell out awkwardly at the time – I'll relate the whole to you when we have more leisure. I think there's one more inquiry which I may be able to pursue on your behalf, too. But there's no time for more now – here comes my next partner – I'll call upon you soon, Justin.'

He was not quite sure whether this constituted a promise or a threat. He passed on to his next partner, who chanced to be Lucy Velmond herself.

She was inclined to be nervous with him at first but he soon put her at ease by talking on trivial subjects in his usual amusing style until at last she was actually laughing.

'May I prevail upon you to present me to Mrs Bradfield as a desirable partner?' he requested, towards the conclusion of the dance. 'That is, if I haven't trodden too often on your toes, of course?'

She looked surprised. 'Why, certainly. Did not George introduce you to her earlier?'

'Yes, but the lady has been engaged for every dance so far, except this one. Now she's chatting to Lady Quainton, so perhaps your combined good offices may suffice to persuade her to take the floor with me for the next.'

Lucy was at a loss to understand why he should particularly wish to partner Mrs Bradfield, a sufficiently good-looking young matron, it was true, but scarcely a dasher; nevertheless, she was anxious to do anything possible for one who had taken such a sympathetic interest in her own wretched plight and soon arranged matters.

Mrs Bradfield appeared flattered to be asked to stand up with one of the most interesting young bachelors in the room and determined to do her best to entertain him. He found her an agreeable chatterbox, and quickly turned this to his advantage by skilfully steering the conversation into the most useful channels for his purpose.

He asked about her neighbours in the country and was told that Sir Rupert and Lady Wingrave were the nearest and most valued of these.

'Dearest Maria Wingrave and I are quite bosom bows – we couldn't be more intimate were we indeed sisters!' she assured him. 'And our children play so prettily together! You will be acquainted with Maria's mother, Lady Kinver, I dare say, though perhaps not with Maria herself?'

He acknowledged that she was correct in both assumptions, then led her on to gossip about her friend. This she was very ready to do; in consequence, he amassed a great deal of information, most of which he thought would prove worthless. The most vital point did not, of course, emerge.

After a while he managed to turn the conversation yet again, this time to the excellent land agent whom her husband had once mentioned.

'Oh, yes, Thompson,' she said. 'Indeed, I do not know how

my husband would go on without him, he's so reliable in every possible way. Poor man, it's melancholy that he should have been disappointed in his family! But so it often is – the most praiseworthy people beget good-for-nothing sons.'

Justin metaphorically pricked up his ears.

'You are quite right, ma'am,' he agreed sententiously. 'May one inquire as to the younger Thompson's fault?'

'Oh, his father scrimped and saved to get the boy a good education, so Bradfield tells me, and then what does he do but fling it all away to go and join a troupe of travelling players! And from that day to this, poor Thompson has never heard a word from his son and has no notion of his whereabouts, nor whether he is still alive! Can you imagine such unfilial behaviour?'

Stifling a yawn, Justin agreed that he could not. He was not sorry when the dance shortly came to an end. Nevertheless, Mrs Bradfield had certainly provided him with food for thought.

For the moment duty was done. He passed on thankfully to his next partner, a friend of Anthea's on whom his appreciative eye had been lingering whenever he dared to spare a glance. She had auburn hair, green eyes, a graceful figure and the most enchanting dimple in her chin.

He sighed and reminded himself sternly of Parson's Mousetrap, the aim of all nubile females and a hazard he was determined at present to avoid.

Chapter XIII

Lucy and Anthea had not met so frequently of late. Since Velmond's reconciliation with his wife he had spent far more time at her side. This was at once a delight and a torment to her, as she tried to explain to her friend when they were able to enjoy a tête-à-tête on the day following the ball.

'It could be oh, so, wonderful!' she said sadly. 'But I cannot enjoy his company while I realize that I am still living a lie. You see, he now believes that story I told him to account for my visit to the pawnbroker's – he begged me to forgive him for ever doubting my word. I, to forgive him! I feel the lowest creature in nature, Anthea.'

'But, my dear Lucy, you must tell him the truth and then all will be comfortable again,' urged Anthea in a reasoning tone.

Lucy sighed despairingly.

'Don't you suppose that's just what I wish with all my heart to do? But how can I possibly begin? Am I to say that the whole was a tissue of lies, just as he supposed in the first place? How can he ever believe anything I say again if I shatter this new-found trust of his? Oh, believe me,' – bowing her head in her hands – 'I've cudgelled my wits for some opening remark that will lead on to a revelation of the truth without causing a permanent breach between us, a situation worse than the former one. I lie awake at nights thinking it out, without ever finding a solution. I feel near demented with worry!'

Anthea was momentarily at a loss. She had never yet experienced the pangs of love and so found it difficult to realize what a sensitive condition it was and how it could lead lovers to behave in what to an onlooker seemed an absurdly irrational manner. Direct and courageous herself, she could only by a wide stretch of her active imagination put herself in the more timid Lucy's place.

'Someone once said that the worst vice is advice,' she said at length lightly, 'so I won't attempt to offer you any, my love. But cheer up, for I feel sure a suitable opportunity will present itself before long. It must be so. Husband and wife living together under one roof cannot possibly persist in misunderstanding each other.'

Lucy was not at all certain of this, but she nodded dolefully. Anthea hastened to change the subject.

'There were one or two questions I wished to ask you on behalf of my Uncle Justin, should you not object,' she continued briskly. 'He wondered if perhaps at any time you'd confided your secret to Dr Wetherby?'

Lucy started. 'Dr Wetherby? Does he think . . . surely he cannot possibly believe that the doctor has anything to do with this monstrous business?'

'It's only sensible to suspect everyone who was present when the murdered man uttered his remarks about Thompson, whom we now know to be a blackmailer,' explained Anthea.

'Yes, but – a doctor!' objected Lucy.

'Even doctors are subject to human fallibility, don't you agree? But I don't think Justin's suspicions are directed specifically at Dr Wetherby, if that consoles you at all. It's simply that he needs to know exactly who could have been aware of your secret. You must see that only someone who knew of it could have used it against you.'

Lucy nodded. 'Well, Cecilia Cleveland – Lady Barclay, as she now is – *did* know, of course, as she was at school with me. I suppose she would have told her parents, so they too would know. But as to Dr Wetherby, I have never confided in him. Unless in some way . . . ' her voice trailed off uncertainly – 'he might have learned something from Mrs Cleveland.'

'Of course, how idiotish I am!' exclaimed Anthea. 'Mrs Cleveland is one of those incurable gossips. When you first came as Velmond's bride to Town, it would not be at all wonderful if she dropped some hint which could have been followed up by that unscrupulous creature, your blackmailer. By the way, Lucy, I think there can be no harm in your knowing that *you* are not the only victim.'

Lucy exclaimed in horror.

'Yes, it *is* frightful, is it not? But at least it may console you a little to learn that you're not alone in your plight. I'm not at liberty to divulge the other victim's name, as you'll readily understand. But perhaps now you'll see why it's important to inform Justin of anything at all which can possibly assist him to discover the miscreant and put an end to his machinations.'

Lucy shuddered. 'Oh, yes – yes, indeed! It's all too monstrous – horrible, horrible!'

She pulled herself together after a moment.

'But I can't recollect anything else which could help Mr Rutherford,' she continued, her brows creased in thought. 'I told him all that I could during our conversation together and I answered all his questions as fully as possible. As to Dr Wetherby,' – she paused momentarily – 'it could be as you suggest. Mrs Cleveland may have let something slip out. I certainly did not tell him myself.'

Anthea seemed satisfied with this and moved on to another matter which was puzzling her.

'I wonder,' she said ruminatively, 'just how it was that Yarnton came to know of this blackmailer? *You* had not previously told anyone of the letter you received and it seems that the other victim was likewise discreet. Of course, Yarnton was the kind of person who made a point of searching out the secrets of others, but the blackmailer has taken care to cover his tracks so thoroughly that even my astute relative – and he *is* more than common clever, you know! – cannot so far discover him. I suppose there wasn't any way in which Yarnton could have known of your predicament? He *did* see you go to the pawnshop, recollect. Could he possibly have discovered the reason for that visit?'

Lucy shook her head.

'Oh, no, how could he? Even if he went into the shop after I had left, and inquired what I was doing there – '

'Which you may be sure he did, on some pretext,' put in Anthea.

'Even so, he could not possibly find out *why* I was selling the necklace,' pointed out Lucy.

'True.'

Anthea still looked thoughtful.

'There's only one thing,' said Lucy doubtfully. 'You may recall that I told you I handed the packet for Thompson to the postman personally? Well, now I come to think of it – for I was agitated at the time, as you will readily understand – that man Yarnton was strolling past, nearby. Only I did not dare to linger but fled back indoors and shut myself away in my room to recover. But I don't quite see how he could possibly make anything of that, do you?'

'*Do I not?*' demanded Anthea excitedly. 'When he had observed you only a short time before at the pawnbroker's? It was the same day, I presume, for I remember your telling Justin that you sent the money off at once?'

Lucy nodded.

'Well then,' declared Anthea triumphantly. 'He followed you home, I expect, then hung about to see what else you might do to add colour to his nasty little scandal. Seeing you hand a packet to the postman he would be quite capable of managing to get a peep at it and observe the direction written on it. And then – and then – why, yes! Perhaps he watched at the Chancery Lane office until someone came to collect that same packet. Then he would know who Thompson was and doubtless guess the truth, or something close enough to it to use as a weapon in his campaign of malice!'

'It may be so and I'm sure you're very clever to think of it, Anthea. But I still don't see how it would assist Mr Rutherford in finding out who this odious creature can be, do you?'

Anthea's face fell. 'No,' she admitted reluctantly. 'Neither do I. And although Justin doesn't know that Yarnton saw you hand the packet to the postman, I dare say he's worked out for himself just how it might have been possible for Yarnton to find out about Thompson. But at least he may not have realized that Dr Wetherby could have learned of your secret through Mrs Cleveland's tattling, for he doesn't know that female as we do – as I do, at all events. Oh, how I do wish, Lucy, that I could take a more active part in assisting him! It's so tiresome at times to be a female, don't you think?'

This was obviously a point of view that had never crossed Lucy's mind before; but she nevertheless dutifully assented.

'I think possibly I may be able to dispense with your services for a few days, Peyton,' Cleveland said to his secretary that same afternoon. 'There's nothing that urgently concerns me going on in the House at present, so I thought of joining my wife in Norfolk. I dare say you'll be glad of a few days' holiday.'

Peyton appeared surprised. 'You are very good, sir, but I do not find my duties onerous. And I had the impression that there were one or two matters – '

Cleveland waved the rest of the sentence away.

'Pooh, nothing that can't wait. Your devotion to duty is exemplary, my dear fellow, but I trust I'm not the kind of employer who keeps the noses of his staff constantly to the grindstone. All work and no play, you know,' he added in a jovial tone. 'Your family must be wishing to see you again, I'm sure.'

'I visited them at Christmas, sir.'

'That's over three months since. Dammit, boy, you sound as reluctant to take a holiday as most men to resume work after one! Is there no pretty female in your neighbourhood at home to whom you're anxious to return, even if filial duty fails to call you there?'

Peyton smiled. 'None that I can recall, sir.'

Cleveland gave him a curious glance. He was not a man who concerned himself greatly with those who served him, but occasionally he did indulge a fleeting speculation as to how this model secretary of his passed his spare time. He knew little of Roderick Peyton's background, for the family connection with Sophia Cleveland was very slight. The young man's mother was a distant cousin of some kind, Cleveland understood, though he had never troubled himself to untangle the precise relationship. A nearer relative had solicited Sophia's benevolence on Roderick Peyton's behalf; and she had promptly seized what appeared to be a heaven-sent opportunity to provide her husband with a much-needed secretary at low cost.

'Wouldn't surprise me to learn that there's no shortage of 'em, where you're concerned,' he said with a rare venture into intimacy.

'Thank you, sir, but you flatter me. I am more concerned with making my way in the world at present, however, rather than branching out in the petticoat line.'

'Quite right, quite right,' approved Cleveland, regretting his impulse towards informality. 'Well, you may pack up and take yourself off this evening, if you wish. I have an engagement which will keep me out until the small hours, so I'll start for Norfolk in the morning.'

He nodded and was turning away to quit the room when Peyton checked him diffidently.

'Beg pardon, Mr Cleveland, but when would you wish me to return?'

Cleveland looked nonplussed for a moment.

'Ah, yes, now let me see. Today's Thursday, is it not? Shall we say on Monday evening or Tuesday? That should do.'

Peyton bowed. 'You are very good, sir,' he repeated.

'Not at all. Goodbye, my dear fellow, and do contrive to amuse yourself.'

He closed the door. Peyton continued to stand beside his desk, his brow creased in thought.

Was Cleveland truly intending to join his wife at their daughter's place in Norfolk? He doubted it. Two and a half years living in the household had shown him that they were far from being a closely united family. Husband and wife quarrelled constantly, mostly about the latter's extravagance. As for that little minx Cecilia, she had been glad enough to quit the family roof for an establishment of her own last autumn. It was scarcely to be expected that she would be devoted to her parents, since she had spent most of her time away at school in Bath except for the year before her marriage.

But if Cleveland were not going to Norfolk, then what else had he in mind? A mistress, perhaps? Peyton shrugged; unlikely. He knew a great deal about his employer's concerns and not only the professional matters which would naturally be his proper province. He had never come across any hint of an amorous connection, though.

There was one other possibility that occurred to him. He considered it for a few minutes, then nodded, satisfied.

He began to go through the papers on his desk, sorting them

methodically, filing some and dealing with others. He was not the kind of man who could leave his effects in a muddle.

That done, he straightened up and gave some thought to what he should do with his unexpected holiday. One thing was certain; he would not be going home to visit his family. He had quitted them without regret on going up to Cambridge six years ago and had rarely been back since. The house was small and uncomfortable, full of younger half-brothers and sisters all falling over each other, and his stepmother was a feckless housekeeper. There was no love lost between his father and himself either, so that it had been a mutual relief when his grandfather had left a small legacy to enable Roderick to go to Cambridge. The Clevelands knew little of this, for they did not concern themselves with him. He had no illusions about their reasons for giving him employment.

There were several ways in which he could usefully spend the time, he decided. For one thing, he would pay a visit to the theatre this evening.

Chapter XIV

The performance at the Olympic theatre had not gone well that evening. Necessary but unfortunate economies in the wardrobe department had literally forced the leading lady – a buxom if handsome female – into a costume several sizes too small. Having deplored this fact at some length at the full pitch of her trained voice, she finally condescended to go on stage, like the experienced trouper she was.

During the first part of her performance she contrived reasonably well by taking small, mincing steps and being careful never to expand her lungs. The audience soon noticed this and showed its disapprobation by means of catcalls and orange peel. In desperation she gave an over-enthusiastic rendering of the heartbreaking scene where she was parted for ever from her child. Not hearts, but her bodice, broke asunder, and she was obliged to continue with both hands clasped affectingly over the rift.

The audience loved this, responding with hearty laughter and a stamping of feet. Driven from the stage Eliza Nympsfield collapsed in her dingy dressing-room in floods of angry tears. The curtain was lowered and a timorous Harlequin thrust from behind it with instructions to keep the audience happy.

The unfortunate Eliza was still giving an enraged private performance backstage to a propitiatory audience of the manager, the wardrobe mistress, some lesser members of the company, a couple of stage hands and the call boy, when a welcome diversion was created by the arrival of the actress's gentleman friend.

He was a stockily-built man whose face suggested that he brooked no nonsense; he had a square jaw and beetling eyebrows over a pair of shrewd grey eyes. His dress, though fashionable, was unostentatious, in the tradition of that arbiter of sartorial taste, Beau Brummell.

A few quiet words from him soon sent the other members of the company away, leaving him alone with Eliza. She abated her histrionics somewhat, but still insisted on pouring out her woes. He nodded from time to time sympathetically; but eventually succeeded in giving her thoughts a new direction by producing a jeweller's case, like a conjurer's rabbit from a hat, and setting it down before her on the spotted and scratched dressing table.

She picked it up quickly, stopping in mid-sentence.

'For me?' she asked in her best stage manner.

He nodded, moving to stand behind her as she turned towards the discoloured mirror.

'For the most beautiful actress to adorn any theatre,' he responded, well within the script. 'Only say that you like it, my dear.'

She opened the case and gave a genuine gasp of admiration. Inside reposed a pendant necklace of gold filigree set with emeralds, rubies and diamonds. She lifted it out and held it against her neck, admiring the gleam and glitter of the stones in the candlelight.

He leaned forward and fastened the clasp, watching as she turned her head this way and that, fascinated.

While she revelled in the sensuous beauty of the necklace, her thoughts were busy. This piece must have cost a fortune and he had not known her for very long. He bid fair to be more rewarding than the string of gentlemen who had sought and won her favours in the past. Might it not be advantageous to renounce her stage career, which had never attained the first flight, and place herself permanently under his protection? But a lifetime of looking out for herself urged caution – besides, he had not yet suggested such a step. Men were notoriously fickle and the Town abounded in ladybirds. A few valuable pieces of jewellery such as this – she had one or two similarly acquired though not quite so expensive already in her possession – were a safer insurance against a rainy day than a premature retirement from her profession in favour of a protector who might withdraw his expensive gifts once he was sure of her.

She turned a smiling face towards him, her ill-humour quite banished.

'Like it – I quite dote on it!' she assured him. 'How you do spoil poor little me, to be sure!'

'Pah, a mere bagatelle,' he replied with a dismissive sweep of his hand. 'Should you like it if we went to the supper party in Hertford Street?'

The house in Hertford Street was the residence of Fanny, sister of Harriette Wilson, the fashionable courtesan. Her champagne and chicken suppers were well known among the demi-reps and their gentlemen. The latter were usually members of the *ton* and they found the free manners and uninhibited behaviour obtaining at these suppers infinitely more to their taste than the formality of Almack's or the drawing-rooms of the fashionable London hostesses.

She accepted this suggestion enthusiastically. Soon she was changed, powdered, perfumed, and with the magnificent necklace prominently displayed by a dashingly décolleté gown of rose silk, she accompanied him to the waiting luxurious chaise.

A nondescript figure in a suit of fustian watched from the flagway while the pair settled themselves into the chaise. He overheard the gentleman give the directions to his coachman. In spite of his appearance the loiterer knew very well exactly what company could be found at the house in Hertford Street. He grinned to himself in the shadows. It was safe to assume that the couple would remain there for several hours, thus giving him ample time for the business he had in mind.

He was on the point of turning away to set about this when a man came reeling out of the lighted exit of the theatre. He cannoned into the loiterer, apologizing in slurred accents.

For a moment the watcher caught a good look at his face. The man was still wearing make-up, so evidently was one of the cast. He was in his mid-twenties, fair-skinned with a slightly bulbous nose. His hat was tipped at a perilous angle over one eye.

As soon as he realized the humble station of the person on whom he had wasted an apology, his tone changed.

'Out of the way, fellow,' he amended with a shaky attempt at dignity. 'Give place to your betters!'

The loiterer shrank back quickly, watching the other make his unsteady way along the street. He heard a chuckle from behind him and turned to see the stage doorkeeper about to shut up the theatre for the night.

'Don't ye heed him, cully,' the man said indulgently. 'For one thing, he's half seas over, for another he's naught but a h'extra who've been 'ere no more'n a few months, nor not likely to stay much longer, the drunken sot. Airs and graces enough for a star, has Mr Theobald Treherne. Theobald Treherne, I *don't* think – more likely Bill Smith! I knows his sort!'

The loiterer mumbled some vague reply and turned away. Once the doorkeeper had locked up and extinguished the lights, the street outside the theatre was dark. No one else was about. The man turned a corner, straightened up, and threw about him a gentleman's evening cloak which he had been carrying bundled up under his arm.

Transformed by this garment into a seemingly respectable fare, he had no difficulty in securing a hackney to take him to Harley Street.

Joe Watts had made good use of his acquaintance with the pretty housemaid at the Clevelands' residence to learn quite a bit about the movements of the inmates. He knew that on this particular evening both Cleveland himself and his secretary would be out and were not expected back until after midnight. The servants had been instructed not to wait up and were all planning – so Joe's informant told him – to make an early night of it while they had the chance. As most of them had to be astir by half-past five in the morning this could scarcely be considered surprising. He had also made himself familiar with the layout of the house and knew how to reach Cleveland's study on the ground floor from the backstairs. All that remained for him to do was to lie low in the small garden at the rear of the house until he saw that the lights in the kitchen quarters had been extinguished.

He knew where he could gain an entry to the house through the larder window, which was always left open a few inches at the top. He told himself he must drop a warning about this habit once he had made use of it. It would never do to encourage genuine burglars.

He had prudently provided himself with a small dark lantern, a necessity for this kind of operation, which he fastened to his belt in order to leave both hands free. Climbing stealthily through the larder window was simple enough and fortunately there was no shelf immediately beneath it. He eased back the shutter of his lantern a fraction to give him the benefit of a glimmer of light, then tiptoed across the floor of the larder and cautiously opened the door.

It gave into the kitchen, where the dull glow of a fire banked down for the night relieved the gloom. It was not the first time he had been in these quarters; he crossed confidently but softly to the door leading into a passage beyond, which would bring him to the backstairs.

He crept stealthily up the flight, testing every step as he ascended, like a cat on hot bricks. At the top he paused to listen, darkening his lantern for the moment.

The house was as silent as an empty church.

Encouraged, he showed a light again, moving along the passage until he reached the door of the study.

He entered cautiously, making sure the shutters were closed behind the curtains before he ventured to light the candles in the room. Softly he turned the key in the lock. At least he would have warning should anyone arrive and at a pinch could escape through a window.

There were two pedestal writing desks of mahogany in the room. The smaller would doubtless be used by Peyton. Should there be time, he would also like to examine the contents of that, but Cleveland's was the more important.

There were six drawers in the larger desk. He tugged at them all, discovering two were locked. He made a wry face. Anything of interest was sure to be contained in those two. He could pick the locks – it would not be the first time a Runner had used burglar's tools – but to do so would leave behind evidence of interference. He looked about him. Was there any chance that Cleveland left his keys where his secretary could find them in his absence, or did he habitually carry them about with him? It could well be that there were some papers he would prefer to keep secret even from his secretary.

He crossed to Peyton's writing desk. It had three drawers and a small cupboard, all of which were unlocked. Papers, papers – he flicked impatiently but expertly over files in the drawers, turning at last to the cupboard. Here were stacks of fresh paper and writing materials, a box containing a franking rubber stamp and inkpad, a few personal items. He was about to shut the door, when he caught sight of a hook at the top of the cupboard from which hung two keys.

He seized these, quickly inserting them into the locks of the fastened drawers in the other desk. They turned easily. He gave a grunt of satisfaction.

The feeling soon changed to one of disgust. The contents of the drawers were doubtless highly confidential to the Government but they appeared not to include anything of a personal nature to Cleveland. He closed and locked them again, disappointed, returning the keys to their original place.

When he came back to stand once more before Cleveland's desk, looking at it in a puzzled way, he noticed a faint line across the upper portion of the kneehole section. He bent down to examine this more closely by the light of his lantern, then drew in a sharp breath. He could now just discern the outline of what must be a small drawer, fitted in such a way that it was practically undetectable.

But how to open it? There was no keyhole, nor a handle.

He had heard of secret drawers which could be opened by releasing a hidden spring and feverishly set about looking for such a device. He found it at last more by luck than judgment. Passing his fingers over the surrounding woodwork, he pressed upon one of a series of small carved flowers and the drawer sprang outwards.

It contained a notebook and three or four letters. Watts picked up the notebook first and began to turn the pages slowly. It seemed to be concerned chiefly with financial matters.

At first he was disappointed, scrutinizing the accounting of purely domestic concerns such as the amounts raised by a sale of horses at Tattersall's. Bearing in mind the lost opportunity with Yarnton's notebook, however, he persevered, turning page after page.

Presently his eyes gleamed with excitement. Here was evidence, right enough, and he intended to impound the book. He thrust it in his pocket.

He turned his attention next to the letters. Only one was of interest to him.

It was composed of words cut from newsprint.

The foot patrol officer in Piccadilly scrutinized Joe Watts suspiciously as a matter of course but did not challenge the Runner as he turned into Albemarle Street. Arrived at Justin Rutherford's house, Watts fitted a key into the lock and quietly admitted himself. It had been previously arranged that Justin's servants should be sent to bed, out of the way.

A light was burning in the hall and Justin emerged from the library to beckon him into the room. He waved the Runner to a chair, handed him a glass of wine poured from a decanter on a side table, then raised his brows interrogatively.

'We've got him, guv'nor!' exclaimed Watts, having taken a gulp at the wine.

He set down his glass and produced the notebook and letter from his pocket.

'What d'you reckon to that, sir, eh?'

Justin took the documents, examining the letter first. Seeing its composition he whistled, then studied the wording attentively for several minutes: 'As usual, £2,000 to Mr Thompson at the Fleet Street office by April eleventh. *Fail at your peril.*'

He turned the single sheet over.

'There's no direction written on it.'

'Reckon he hadn't got as far as that yet,' replied Watts, having drained his wine glass. 'Just finished putting it together, I'd opine. And if you'll take a look at this entry in the notebook, sir,' – he took it from Justin's hand to find the relevant page, then gave it back to him – 'you'll see there's further evidence. Not but what the letter's damning enough, by all accounts.'

Justin set down the letter in order to examine the notebook.

The page to which Watts had turned bore no heading and there were only four entries:

1814, October	£2,000	Reading
1815, April	£2,000	Islington
1815, October	£2,000	Charing X
1816, April		

The final entry was incomplete.

He looked up, frowning.

'Well?' demanded Watts triumphantly.

'Very well,' replied Justin slowly. 'All the same, I do wonder why he didn't keep a record of the earlier payments.'

'Earlier payments?'

'Yes. Lady Kinver stated that she had been making six-monthly payments of two thousand pounds regularly ever since October of 1811. Now, why do you suppose Cleveland should omit those before the first date shown here?'

Watts shrugged. 'He may not have bothered to keep a reckoning at first. If you notice, sir, all the other financial transactions in this here book date from about two years back.'

Justin turned over the other pages and nodded.

'Yes, that's so,' he agreed.

'Then, with respect, sir, I can't see it signifies. There's enough evidence here to bring him into Bow Street for questioning.'

'Yes, I think we must certainly question him, though the answers may not be quite what we expect. You'll go there for him tomorrow, I take it?'

'Soon as I can get a warrant signed, sir. Well, I suppose after that there's not much point in asking how you fared at the doctor's place?'

'Nevertheless, I'll tell you. I found ample evidence that over the past four years Dr Wetherby has had a succession of expensive ladybirds in keeping. The latest is an actress at the Olympic Theatre and she left there after the performance this evening in his company. She was wearing a fortune round her neck in the shape of a jewelled necklace. I saw the invoice for it in his bureau, later.'

Watts whistled. 'So he has good reason for raising the wind

by blackmail too, and we *think* he may be in the know about Lady Velmond, as well as t'other poor creature whom he does definitely know about. Pity he's out of the running, as we've nailed our man.'

Justin gave a sceptical grin. 'Ever heard that proverb about not counting your chickens?'

Sir Nathaniel Conant was seriously disturbed at the prospect of bringing in a member of His Majesty's Government to Bow Street for questioning.

'You must effect the arrest as discreetly as possible,' he warned Watts. 'In the eventuality of there being any error, I shudder to think of the repercussions as far as this office is concerned. It is a thousand pities that Mr Rutherford himself cannot handle this in a more private way.'

'But there's evidence enough, sir, of the MP's guilt,' persisted Watts. 'We can't let him get away with it, now, can we?'

'No, no, of course not. But if you could perhaps prevail upon Mr Rutherford to go along with you and see what can be done to manage the business without making too much stir? One does not like to trespass on his time – such an influential family – but then, dealing with a Member of Parliament – '

'Lor' bless you, sir,' said Watts cheerfully, 'Captain Rutherford – I should say Mr – will make nothing of a little job like that, I'll be bound. He'll come with me, right enough.'

Thus reassured, Sir Nathaniel issued the required warrant. Watts went hot-foot to Albemarle Street. He found Justin quite agreeable to accompanying him on his errand.

'Naturally, I didn't consider I should interfere in the official part of this affair, Joe, but since your chief asks it, I'll be relieved to have a word with Cleveland myself,' said Justin. 'And to be present also at the official interrogation – if it comes to that.'

'Which it most certainly will, sir,' insisted Watts.

Arrived at Cleveland's house Justin handed in his card at the door; a measure they had agreed upon in advance as meeting Sir Nathaniel Conant's request for discretion. The butler looked surprised. It was not yet ten o'clock in the morning, an hour well in advance of that usual for the Quality to pay calls upon each other.

'I regret, sir, that Mr Cleveland is not at home,' the man said formally.

Justin gave him a quizzical look. 'Perhaps not,' he said gently, but with quiet authority. 'Nevertheless, I believe he will see me if you inform him that it is upon a matter of the utmost urgency.'

'Oh, dear, I fear I have not made myself quite clear, Mr Rutherford,' replied the butler apologetically. 'When I informed you that Mr Cleveland was not at home, I meant that he has gone away. He left for Norfolk less than an hour since and is not expected to return for several days.'

Watts stifled an exclamation.

'I see,' said Justin. 'Then I would like to speak with Mr Cleveland's secretary, please.'

The butler shook his head. 'Mr Peyton has been given leave during Mr Cleveland's absence, sir, and he also quitted the house early this morning.'

'Then perhaps you'll be good enough to tell me whereabouts in Norfolk I may reach Mr Cleveland,' replied Justin. 'It is, as I said, a matter of urgency.'

The butler was not particularly alarmed by this statement, used as he was to callers desirous of consulting his employer on parliamentary business. He opened the door wider.

'If you will be pleased to enter, Mr Rutherford, I will write down the direction for you. Mr Cleveland is to join Mrs Cleveland at the house of their daughter, Lady Barclay.'

As Justin was about to step inside, Watts touched his arm. 'See you outside in a few moments,' he said *sotto voce*.

Justin nodded. When he descended the steps into St James's Square after obtaining the information he needed, there was no sign of the Runner. He strolled slowly along and presently Watts joined him, emerging from the mews of the house a trifle out of breath and looking disturbed.

'All poppycock, sir – this going to Norfolk, I mean! Had a word with my little housemaid and she's friendly with one o' the grooms. Seems Cleveland told this fellow at the last moment to be ready to accompany him in his curricle – where

124

d' you think, sir? – to Dover! Skipping the country for France, that's what, I opine. Any hope of catching him, d' you reckon?'

'We'll have a damn good try! Whistle up that hack of yours and we'll get back to my place. I've a pair of blood cattle in my stables should show a clean pair of heels to anything of Cleveland's, by all I've heard. But he'll have pretty well an hour's start of us.'

'If he does intend crossing the Channel, there'll be some delay in booking a passage and then waiting on the tide,' mused Watts. 'Likely we'll get him at Dover.'

With the minimum of delay they were presently bowling along the road towards Greenwich and Dartford in Justin's lightly sprung, smart curricle. At Dartford they changed horses, leaving Justin's greys in the charge of his groom until the return journey. While the change was being made they heard from an ostler that their quarry had also stopped there about half an hour since.

'There's a sporting chance we might pick him up at Rochester,' declared Justin. 'That's if this pair can stand the pace. They're not bad,' he added, flicking his whip at them. 'Not in the same class as my greys, of course, but one don't expect that of job cattle.'

The horses were fresh, however, and acquitted themselves creditably, covering the thirteen miles to the Bull at Rochester in less than an hour. Justin drove through the archway into the cobbled courtyard. An ostler came running at once.

Watts questioned the man while Justin strode into the inn with the object of taking a quick pull at a tankard of ale before continuing their journey. He had just reached the counter in the taproom when Watts appeared at his elbow, drawing him to one side.

'Our man's here,' he said in an undertone, 'stopped off to get a bite to eat. I'll have a word with the landlord, see just where we'll find him. I told 'em in the yard not to put our horses to yet awhile.'

Justin nodded. 'Devil take the fellow! I'm parched with thirst and I'll wager you are, too. However, duty calls, let's see mine host.'

They elicited the information that Cleveland could be found

in a private room upstairs, number six. Accordingly they mounted the broad staircase which led to galleries of bedrooms and private sitting-rooms, soon locating the one they sought.

Watts rapped smartly on the door and, without waiting for an answer, walked in purposefully, closely followed by Justin.

Cleveland was sitting there alone at a small table on which were the remains of a meal. He had half risen at the knock and now straightened himself, staring as they entered.

'Who in thunder – ?' he began.

Watts produced his official baton, displaying the crown stamped on the top of it.

'Bow Street, sir. I'd like you to accompany me back to London for questioning.'

'The devil you would!'

He took a longer look at Watts, then snorted.

'Aren't you that officer who came to my house to ask some stupid question or other not more than a week since?' he demanded.

'The same. Joseph Watts, sir.'

'Well, Watts,' continued Cleveland, 'I can only repeat what I told you at the time. I consider that I've been pestered more than enough over this business and must warn you that any more harassment on your part will cost you your office.' He turned to Justin. 'As for you, Mr Rutherford, I am not perfectly clear as to what I owe the unsolicited honour of your company?'

Justin bowed. 'That will emerge, Mr Cleveland. Indeed, I may say that you could be grateful for my presence here, little as you think it now.'

'Indeed?' Cleveland sneered. 'You will oblige me by leaving this room immediately, sir, and taking your henchman with you.'

'Not so fast,' put in Watts grimly. 'I have a warrant here for your arrest, Mr Henry Cleveland, and I advise you to come quietly.'

Cleveland's face paled slightly and he leaned on the back of his chair for support. For a moment he said nothing.

'I don't need to ask on what charge,' he said at last in an altered voice.

'Don't you, sir?' demanded Watts. 'That saves a mort o'

time, then, don't it? Just you come along.'

Justin raised a hand to stop them as Cleveland took a few hesitant steps to Watts's side.

'One moment,' he said. 'There are certain misunderstandings which need clearing up first. You say you know what the charge is, Cleveland. Oblige us by stating it.'

Watts opened his mouth to interrupt but Justin silenced him with a gesture.

'What the devil's the good of that?' asked Cleveland wearily. 'It's that Stock Exchange fraud business, isn't it? When Cochrane was convicted two years ago, I thought myself safe – after all, I didn't make as much out of it as Cochrane and his brother – a paltry sum by their standards. And after a lapse of two years since the conviction of the principals in the affair, who'd have supposed the Stock Exchange would trouble further? I might have known, though – just my luck. In view of everything, it can't signify greatly.' He sighed.

'No, I don't believe it does,' replied Justin quietly. 'But I must put you right on this point, Cleveland, the charge brought against you is not one of fraud.'

Cleveland stared. 'Not? Then what, in God's name?'

'Blackmail,' stated Watts. 'We're in possession of evidence. And leading from that, suspicion of the murder of Marmaduke Yarnton.'

'*Blackmail!*' Cleveland choked on the word. 'I – a blackmailer? Oh, God, what a tangle! And murder – why should *I* be suspected of murdering Yarnton? I'd got nothing against the man. Didn't like him, but who did? Hell and the devil, you've got it all wrong, man, I swear!'

'Yes, so I thought,' said Justin. 'Let's sit down for a moment, shall we, while we straighten things out? And I think perhaps, Cleveland' – as the other sank into his chair thankfully, looking as if his legs would no longer support him – 'you'd be the better for finishing the glass of wine we interrupted.'

Watts frowned at his partner as they both seated themselves on two chairs placed round the table. He could not entirely approve of Justin Rutherford's manner of conducting this interview, much as he trusted his former captain. Nevertheless he waited in silence while they watched Cleveland toss down the wine.

'You'll recall, no doubt,' began Justin, opening the batting, as he put it to himself, 'that Officer Watts questioned you a week since about Yarnton's mention of a man named Thompson?' Cleveland nodded but said nothing. 'That reference of Yarnton's seemed to produce a strong reaction in more than one of his hearers,' continued Justin. 'We have since discovered why. Thompson is the pseudonym of a blackmailer.'

'But – but how – who – ?' stuttered Cleveland.

'I collect you mean how do we know? Simply this – one of the blackmailer's victims confided in a friend, who brought the information to me – with permission, of course, knowing that I was attempting to solve the mystery of Yarnton's murder. What I was seeking to establish was a strong enough *motive* for the deed – the opportunity was open to almost every male present at that soirée, while the means were to hand – if you'll forgive a somewhat grim pun. But once we knew Thompson to be a blackmailer, the motive became clear. Yarnton's reference to the name implied that he knew the real identity of the blackmailer and that it was one of the guests among the group to whom he mentioned Thompson. *You* were one of that number.'

'Yes, but I'm not the man! You can't bring this home to me!' Cleveland's voice mounted almost to a pitch of hysteria.

Watts rose from his chair and slapped down on the table the notebook and letter he had taken from the secret drawer.

'There's the evidence, Mr Cleveland. Deny it if you can. The letter speaks for itself and a page in the book records your transactions. I think you'd best come along o' me to Bow Street without more ado.'

Cleveland stared at the documents, amazed.

'So that's where they are! I feared the worst when I discovered they were missing this morning – it finally decided me to clear out. But you're on the wrong track, I tell you! I'm not Thompson – far otherwise! *I'm* the one who's being black-mailed – have been ever since the Stock Exchange business and I can't find the ready any longer! I'm at a stand!'

Justin nodded. 'I thought that was it,' he said quietly.

Watts turned a surprised look on him.

'You did, sir? But I don't see that – we've only his word for it.' He tapped the evidence lying on the table. 'This letter's plain enough and then the entries in the book – '

'Which are incomplete,' pointed out Justin, 'in the light of what we know about the blackmailer's transactions.'

Cleveland had bowed his head in his hands while this interchange was taking place; but now he roused himself.

'I can prove that I've paid out the amounts recorded in the book,' he said heavily. 'You can check that at my banker's. He'll also show you that I've precious little standing to my credit – certainly not the account of a successful blackmailer.'

He gave a harsh laugh.

Watts considered this for a moment. If true it would substantiate Cleveland's story; unless, of course, he had another account elsewhere under a false name. There remained the letter, however.

'And what about this letter, sir?' he demanded, pointing to the document.

'I received that yesterday. It's exactly like all the others which came to me at six-monthly intervals, except that the receiving office was a different one each time.'

'But it's not directed to you,' said Justin.

'It was folded in a covering sheet which I burnt – foolishly, as it now appears, but I was enraged at the time.'

'Then why didn't you destroy the whole?'

'Because I needed to be sure which receiving office was stated, as he varied them. I hadn't quite made up my mind then that I was going to make a run for it to France without attempting to try and raise the blood money. Later, I realized it was the only way, God help me!'

'Suppose we accept your story for the present, Cleveland,' said Justin. 'Have you any notion who this man Thompson could be?'

Cleveland gave a hopeless shrug.

'The most obvious suspect seemed to me to be either my broker or someone connected with the Stock Exchange. When I received the first demand I tried watching at the post office where I'd been instructed to send the money, but it was an impossible task. I couldn't be there all the time and there was no means of knowing exactly when he would collect after the due date. Moreover, what good would it have done me to know who he was? I couldn't bring him to book without ruining my reputation – the only thing was to pay.'

'A melancholy situation indeed. I'd like to have the name of your broker. Perhaps you'd be good enough to write it on the back of this card?'

He handed a visiting card to Cleveland, who obeyed.

'And now what's to become of me?' asked Cleveland with a grim look about his mouth.

'I think it will be necessary for you to accompany this officer to Bow Street to explain matters to the chief magistrate,' replied Justin. 'I suggest you inform your groom that you've changed your plans and instruct him to convey your vehicle home without you. You will then travel back with us.'

'And afterwards?'

'That will depend, I imagine, on whether the Stock Exchange chooses to prosecute. But in the meantime, you can render valuable assistance to the police which may mitigate your offence. I'll explain more fully when we reach Bow Street.'

Chapter XVI

Justin called at his brother's house in Berkeley Square on the following day.

'Look here, old fellow,' said Edward when they managed to find a few moments alone in the library, 'have you got any further with this investigation of yours? I can't help thinking about what you said – suspects, y'know – and I keep looking askance at 'em whenever they come in my way. I can only hope to God they don't notice! One thing, though, Velmond don't seem to be under suspicion any longer. He's looking remarkably cheerful lately.'

'Yes, there can no longer be any reason for the authorities to suspect him. As for progress, I believe I can claim that the ground is gradually being cleared. You may recall that I suggested in the beginning that there might be other victims of this blackmailer? We now know of one other, at least – possibly two.'

'Good God! Do you intend to tell me who they are?'

Justin nodded. 'Since I've confided in your daughter, I can scarce draw the line at you, what? The second victim is Lady Kinver.'

'*Lady Kinver?*' repeated Lord Rutherford, in tones of horror. 'My dear chap, are you sure? If ever any female could claim to have lived a life of complete rectitude – apart from my own female relatives, of course,' he added hastily, 'she must be the one! And as for poor Kinver, his health was such before he died that there was small possibility of his getting into any kind of scandal. It seems incredible, Justin!'

'Nevertheless, it is so. I have it from Lady Kinver herself, through the medium of my godmama, I must add, a very useful witness.'

'Cassandra? Ah, there's not much goes on but Cassie knows

of it, true enough. Well, who'd have thought it?'

'It's only fair to admit, old chap, that your judgment of character isn't at fault,' said Justin with a grin. 'The scandal didn't concern either Jane or Charles Kinver but their daughter Maria.'

Edward drew down his mouth. 'Hm. Don't recollect the chit, though I fancy we attended her wedding – sure to have done, in fact. Poor Jane, nasty business. Children can be the very devil,' he added feelingly. 'Did this blackguard touch her for much blunt?'

'In the region of twenty thousand pounds.'

'Good God!' exclaimed Lord Rutherford again.

'There's a certain monotony in the way you keep calling upon your maker, old fellow,' Justin objected lightly.

'I may well do so! The whole business is fantastic and if anyone other than you had told me of it I should say they were gammoning me,' retorted Edward. 'I can only hope you succeed in putting an end to this scoundrel's activities, for such scum shouldn't be allowed to live – hanging's too good for 'em! Who's the other poor devil? The one you say is a possible victim?'

'Cleveland,' answered Justin briefly.

'But I thought you said he was one of your list of suspects?' protested Edward.

Justin admitted that this was so and went on to explain the situation.

'So you see,' he finished, 'until we've examined his banking account, we cannot be sure that he really did make those payments. For myself, I suspected from quite an early stage that he might be a victim rather than the criminal. When you told me that there were rumours about his connection with the Stock Exchange fraud it did open up such a possibility.'

'The rate you're going, you'll soon find all your suspects are victims,' pronounced Lord Rutherford gloomily. 'Wasn't Bradfield one of 'em? Don't mind telling you, Justin, I don't like that above half, as Anthea's just accepted an invitation to join a small house party at the Bradfields' place in Sussex for a few days. She's off there tomorrow. Not that I think for a moment Bradfield could possibly be this scoundrel Thompson, but then who the devil does seem likely?'

'Quite so. Who else will be in this party?'

'The Velmonds and the Aylesfords, I believe. No others. Anthea never met Mrs Bradfield before the lady's present visit to Town, so we think she's probably being asked because of her friendship with Lucilla Velmond. Poor little Lucy's so shy, Mrs Bradfield may have felt she'd be more comfortable with Anthea along.'

'No one can accuse my niece of being shy,' agreed Justin.

'Good God, no, quite the reverse! Which reminds me, she insists on having a private word with you before you go. I'll send her in here to you, but mind, don't set her on to any freakish starts!'

Justin promised and a few moments later Anthea swept into the library, looking as captivating as usual in a white morning gown of deceptive simplicity. He studied her appreciatively for a moment through his quizzing glass.

'Very charming,' he commented. 'And for whose benefit, may I ask? Not, I fancy, the frog-faced Grassington, your admirer at the ball.'

She laughed musically. 'I'm not expecting to see anyone but family today – it *is* Sunday, recollect.'

'So that's why I wasn't at the necessity of beating a path to your door over the bodies of suitors.'

'You're as absurd as ever,' she chided him. 'But pray attend to me for a moment, Justin, for I've some information to give you, though I fear it's not vastly exciting, being more negative than otherwise. I did ask Lucy if she'd ever confided in Dr Wetherby and she said she had not.'

He nodded. 'It seemed unlikely.'

'Yes, but she did suggest another way in which Dr Wetherby – or possibly others, for that matter – might have heard of her escapade,' went on Anthea in a more hopeful tone. 'You may not be aware of this, Justin, but Mrs Cleveland is a prodigious tattler and she must have known of Lucy's secret through Cecilia. It seems to me quite likely that when Lucy's engagement to Velmond was first talked of in society, dear Mrs Cleveland may have dropped some lightly veiled hint about poor Lucy's past. And then, of course, not only Dr Wetherby

133 of course, not only Dr Wetherby

but anyone else, for that matter, might have come to hear of it. Do you not think that probable?'

'Indeed I do and I can't tell you how prodigiously grateful I am for your invaluable assistance, my dear niece.'

'Pooh, you're roasting me again! But there's another thing, Justin. I believe I've managed to puzzle out how it was that Yarnton came to learn of the existence of this blackmailer Thompson. There's something Lucy told me – '

She proceeded to relate the conversation which had passed between Lucy and herself on this subject.

'Of course, I dare say you'll have already thought of it for yourself,' she concluded a trifle ruefully.

'I wasn't aware that Yarnton had actually observed Lucilla Velmond hand the packet to the postman, so naturally you had the advantage of me in that respect,' he answered in a rallying tone. 'Given that fact, your train of reasoning subsequently appears eminently plausible. I must admit that I'd worked out something of the kind, on a purely hypothetical basis, of course. But that's by the way. And now I think it's time I gave you my latest information, Anthea.'

He told her about Cleveland.

'Oh, but that's a great deal too bad!' she exclaimed at the conclusion. 'I had quite decided, you know, that he was the villain!'

'May I ask why?'

'Woman's intuition!' she laughed. 'And it did seem then that he was the only one who could have known of both secrets, Lucy's *and* Lady Kinver's. Now it appears possible that all the other suspects might have come to know, too. But Justin – '

She broke off and he raised inquiring brows at her.

'If Mr Cleveland is yet another victim, who do you think would be aware of *his* secret?'

'According to Cleveland himself, his broker.'

'Stockbroker, do you mean? But who is he? He cannot be one of your original list of suspects!'

'Not that, no. But he is the same man whom Bradfield employs for his own transactions.'

'Oh!'

'Yes, my girl.' He waved an admonitory finger at her. 'But

134

while you're staying in his house in Sussex, you will contrive to forget about that and all else to do with this affair. Understood?'

She nodded docilely enough; but he did not altogether trust the gleam in her eye which showed for just a second, then was gone.

There were those who disapproved of Sunday travelling but evidently the gentleman who arrived unexpectedly at the Crown in Amersham during the afternoon of that day was not of their number. He had only a manservant with him and had brought one small portmanteau; so it was assumed by mine host, a shrewd judge of travellers, that his visitor would require only overnight accommodation. There seemed some uncertainty about this on the gentleman's part, for he bespoke a private sitting-room as well as bedchambers for himself and his servant. Naturally the landlord did not press him on this point but hastened downstairs to ascertain that a suitably good dinner would be awaiting the guest at the hour requested.

Having left his man Selby to attend to matters at the inn, Justin strolled down the High Street of the attractive little market town. His discerning eye took in the varying styles of architecture, from mediaeval through Tudor to that of the present day. He paused to consider the Market Hall and farther along the neat row of almshouses.

It was just beyond these that he came upon the house he was seeking, an undistinguished building some fifty years old sandwiched between two others of similar vintage. He hesitated outside for a few moments before finally making up his mind and resolutely striding up the path to wield the knocker.

A piece of dimity curtaining was hastily twitched aside and a child's face appeared for a few seconds before vanishing just as suddenly behind an impatient female arm which drew the curtain back into place. The sound of babbling voices reached his ears and there was a quick scurry of feet before the door was finally opened and a diminutive, not very tidy housemaid appeared on the threshold.

She opened the door the merest fraction, looking inquiringly at the visitor but saying nothing.

'I believe this is the residence of the Reverend Josiah Peyton?' asked Justin politely.

She nodded, twisting her apron in her fingers. He began to wonder if she chanced to be deaf, in which case his errand would be even more difficult to explain. At that moment, however, two children came running towards her, and she shooed them away with enough eloquence to dispel this notion.

He had extracted a card from his case and was about to proffer it to her, when a plaintive female voice called out from the regions beyond the hall.

'Who is it, Sally? If it's Mrs Rumford about the hymn books, show her into the parlour, and I will join her in a moment. Oh, you little wretch!'

This last was evidently addressed to one of the children, for the maid appeared unabashed. She accepted the card gingerly, as though expecting it to explode at any minute, and opened the door wider.

'Be pleased to step into the parlour, sir, an' I'll fetch missis.'

The two children had reappeared, bringing two smaller fry with them; but she steered him skilfully past them into the front-room from which he had previously been observed. After some argument with the children she succeeded in sending them off and closing the door upon the visitor.

He looked about him. The furniture and carpet were of good quality, but showed the ravages of time. The hangings could with advantage have been renewed, as the sun had faded their colour. An open pianoforte against one wall had several damaged keys, no doubt as a result of being battered by numerous pairs of inexpert young hands.

The door opened to admit a lady of ample proportions dressed in a lilac gown which Justin's experienced eye noted was several seasons out of date. She looked harassed and the hair under her cap tended to straggle, but her voice was undoubtedly that of a well-bred woman.

'How do you do, Mr, er –' She consulted the card in her hand in a flustered way.

'Rutherford,' he supplied, bowing. 'At your service, ma'am.

136

I believe I am addressing Mrs Peyton?'

She acknowledged this, looking puzzled. Nevertheless she invited him to be seated.

'I don't wish to trespass on your time, ma'am,' he said, remaining on his feet for the moment. 'I really called in hoping to see your husband, the Reverend Josiah Peyton.'

Her face cleared. 'Oh, an acquaintance of Josiah's!' she exclaimed. 'I thought I had never before met you, Mr, er – '

'Rutherford,' said Justin patiently. 'Is your husband at home, ma'am? Do you think he could possibly spare me a moment of his time?'

'He's stepped out for an hour or two, Mr, er – '

'Rutherford.'

'Oh, yes, pray forgive me, I fear I am rather stupid about names and we do have quite a number of callers,' she said, fluttering her hands about in a helpless way. 'But do be seated and I'll send for some refreshment.'

'Pray don't put yourself to that trouble, ma'am. Perhaps I need not await your husband's return, as I dare say you will be able to tell me what I wish to know. It is this, do you expect your son, Mr Roderick Peyton, to pay you a visit? Or perhaps he has already arrived? I inquired for him at Mr Cleveland's residence in London and was told that I might find him here as he had been granted a few days' leave of absence.'

'Roderick?' She pushed some of the straying hair back under her cap in a distrait way. 'Oh, but he is not my son, you know – I am the second Mrs Peyton.'

Justin apologized. She inclined her head in acknowledgment.

'That is quite all right. But he isn't here. Indeed, he rarely visits his father. We've seen very little of him over the years since first he went up to Cambridge.'

Justin was not really surprised to learn this. Unless a strong rapport had existed between father and son, this establishment could have few attractions for any young man.

'So you have no notion, ma'am, where I could find him?'

She shook her head. 'I fear we know nothing of his present life beyond the little he tells his father of his employment, when they *do* chance to meet.' She sniffed. 'I don't scruple to tell you,

Mr, er, er, Rutherford,' – she brought this out triumphantly – 'that it is not *my* notion of a proper filial relationship.'

'Quite so, ma'am,' he replied smoothly. 'But I'll not trouble you any further in this matter. I can readily enough see your stepson on his return to Town. I merely dropped in because I happened to be in the neighbourhood. Your servant, Mrs Peyton.'

He bowed and withdrew with what dignity he could muster among a group of curious, chattering children who came surging forward the moment the parlour door opened.

He adjusted his cravat, which had become slightly askew owing to the jostling of the children, and breathed a sigh of relief as he left the house to walk back to the Crown. Matters had gone more smoothly than he had anticipated. If Peyton had been at home, what possible excuse could have been given for seeking an interview with him here in Buckinghamshire, instead of in Town? The secretary was not quite so gullible as his stepmother, of that Justin was sure.

The real object of the visit had been to discover something about Peyton's background; since Cleveland, when questioned, had shown himself disappointingly ignorant of practically everything concerning his secretary except the whereabouts of his parental home.

Now that Justin had visited that home, it came as no surprise to him that Peyton chose to spend his free time elsewhere. It would perhaps be useful to discover precisely where; Watts might be able to glean some information on that head from the pretty housemaid. Servants always knew everything.

Of course, he reflected later, over an excellent dinner at the Crown, if the plan they had concocted with Cleveland turned up trumps, no further investigation would be necessary, as the blackmailer would perforce reveal himself.

But the habit of disciplined, methodical research would not be set aside. There was one more line of inquiry which he intended to follow up while he was in this county. It would be trickier than anything yet, as he dared not approach the principals in the affair and had no notion who else might possess any information. Added to that, an interval of five years tended to make recollection uncertain. Nevertheless he intended to try his luck in Missenden tomorrow.

He smiled to himself as he held his glass of claret up to the light. He had already formulated a theory about the Thompson affair. It would be interesting to see how close to the truth it turned out to be.

Chapter XVII

*L*ady Kinver sat motionless in front of her bureau, staring at the letter in her hand as though she had never before set eyes on its like, instead of being painfully familiar with such missives over a period of years. It was always the same letter, apart from a variation in the postal receiving office, and it always produced the same effect upon her – shock, horror, confusion of mind.

Presently she rose from her chair to gaze heedlessly through the window, debating what action to take. She had followed her friend Cassie's advice in confiding her trouble to Mr Justin Rutherford, but evidently so far not much good had come of it. She was still receiving demands for blackmail from the unknown Thompson. Who could he be? Who was it who could possibly know of that well-kept, dangerous secret?

A tap upon the door startled her from her reverie. Pulling herself together she crossed quickly to the bureau and stuffed the letter into one of the pigeon holes. Then she called out permission to enter.

'Dr Wetherby has called, milady,' announced a liveried footman.

Lady Kinver hesitated a moment, then said, 'Show him in.'

The doctor entered, bowed, and eyed her with a professional scrutiny.

'How do you find yourself today, my lady?' he asked in bracing tones. 'Much improved, I trust?'

She shook her head, motioning him to a chair as she sat down herself.

'A little, but not much,' she replied in a dispirited tone.

He lifted her hand to take her pulse rate but she pulled it impatiently away.

'It's not a matter of health, but of spirits, doctor.'

'The one often reflects the other, dear lady.' His tone was urbane. 'And pray what is afflicting your spirits, may I ask?'

For a moment she looked him steadily in the eye, almost accusingly.

'I had thought it possible that you would yourself know the answer to that question,' she said acidly.

He raised his bushy eyebrows.

'I, Lady Kinver? It would be of service to us both, if that were so.'

'You cannot pretend to have forgotten the events of that November, six years ago?'

His brows came down in a heavy frown.

'Ah – yes,' he said slowly. 'But that has long since gone by. There is no profit in thinking of the past.'

'There is profit for someone,' she retorted with emphasis. 'Oh, yes, indeed, someone has turned my misery to good account! And that unfortunate creature Yarnton seemed to have a strong notion of the identity of that "someone", too! Have you, Dr Wetherby?'

'My dear Lady Kinver,' he said soothingly, 'it simply will not do to fret yourself into these agitated humours. It is the very worst thing for your depressed condition. Pray be guided by me and lie down upon your bed for an hour or two. I'll send round a sedative immediately.'

'A fig for your sedatives!' she snapped. 'You haven't answered my question!'

'Tut, tut.' His tone was indulgent. 'By all means vent your spleen upon me, my lady, if by so doing you obtain relief. As for your question, a moment's reflection will show you that I cannot answer it.'

'Cannot, or will not?' she said challengingly.

He made no answer but shrugged his heavy shoulders.

'You were the only person other than Nanny Barton to know my secret.'

'A secret which I have kept, my lady.'

His eyes did not waver from hers. Her face crumpled suddenly, the defiance dying out of her expression.

'At a price, Dr Wetherby?'

'No price can be too high for peace of mind, surely, Lady

141

Kinver. And now pray heed my advice – go and rest for a while.'

Justin reached home from his Buckinghamshire visit late on Monday afternoon to find that Watts had called upon him earlier. The Runner had left a note saying that he could be found at the Brown Bear when wanted.

The Brown Bear was a tavern in Bow Street which was known locally as the Russian coffee house. It was frequently used by the Runners for various purposes, occasionally even for housing prisoners overnight until more suitable accommodation could be found for them.

Justin at once dispatched one of his stable boys with a message to this hostelry and by the time he had washed away the dust of travel Watts had arrived in Albemarle Street.

'All's right and tight with Cleveland,' he reported. 'He fell in with our plan – well, not much choice for him, was there, sir? Returned home after the interview at Bow Street and gave it out that he'd been recalled to Town urgently. Nothing for folk to wonder at in that, seeing as he's an MP. We were able to provide him with a wad of counterfeit notes we brought in last week from as neat a forger as we've seen in a long time, gone now to the Nubbing Cheat. He's to send them off to this Thompson at Fleet Street receiving office to arrive by 11 April, as instructed by the demand letter. Agreed to it all, quiet as a lamb.'

Justin nodded. 'Good. We didn't anticipate any difficulty.'

'The eleventh is Friday, sir, so I dare say you'll want me at the Fleet Street office on surveillance from then onwards? After all, this should mean we can nab our man red-handed, so there's not much need to go ferreting out any further clues to his identity.'

'True. From speculation, we move to proof positive, unless matters go awry. Nevertheless I may as well tell you what information I was able to collect on my travels.'

He proceeded to give an amusing account of his visit to the Peyton family home.

Watts laughed. 'No wonder that young cully don't spend his

time there! According to Polly – that's the housemaid at Cleveland's place – he's got a female in Islington, as she's heard him direct a hackney there on a couple of occasions. All the same, these females, sir! Heads stuffed full o' romantical notions – breath o' life to 'em! Not but what she may be in the right of it. He's a handsome young blood, no mistake.'

'Afterwards I took myself off to Missenden, the village where Lady Kinver's sister, Mrs Hardwick, resides,' continued Justin. 'I'd judged it might be tricky to try and discover which families were on visiting terms with the lady five years since, but no such thing! I'd reckoned without meeting the landlady of the King's Arms in the village, one of the most dedicated gossips I've ever encountered and that's a bold word! Without more than the gentlest hint she divulged intimate details of the half dozen or so most prominent families in the neighbourhood.'

'You're not saying she knew about *that* business?' asked Watts, lifting his eyebrows.

Justin shook his head. 'No, but she did know who'd been dangling after whom for the past umpteen years and didn't scruple to make her knowledge public. Much of it was of no interest whatever to me, of course, but she did mention several names besides that of Captain Tilsworth in connection with the Kinver girl.'

'Any of 'em known to us, sir?'

'Not as far as I can tell, but there could be relationships and so on of which we're in the dark at present. One point of interest, though – a lady named Cardross who lives within a few miles of Mrs Hardwick is the elder sister of none other than Velmond's friend Bradfield.'

Watts whistled. 'Was this Mr Bradfield visiting there by any chance while the Kinver young lady was with her aunt?'

'Annoying thing was, I couldn't discover that, try as I might, without appearing to be too interested, for of course my rôle was that of the slightly bored recipient of these unwanted confidences. I did learn that Mr Bradfield doesn't visit his sister as frequently as he used to do before his marriage, as seemingly Mrs Bradfield and Mrs Cardross don't go along harmoniously. The good lady of the inn was a mine of information on such delicate matters. However, I dare say I'll come by that information some other way.'

'That's if it's needed, sir, and I'll lay odds it won't be, now,' said Watts confidently. 'If we can nab our man with the packet directed to Thompson in his possession, we'll have all the proof we need of his guilt.'

'At the risk of your thinking proverbs are my strong suit, Joe, I'll quote you the one about many a slip between cup and lip,' chuckled Justin. 'Besides, there's still the satisfaction of working out the puzzle for oneself. Who would you select from our list of suspects to put your money on, what?'

'A few days since, I'd have said Cleveland,' replied Watts promptly. 'Seemed to fit the case on all points. Now, of course, he's cleared, or at least he should be when his banker's confirmed his statement, which Sir Nathaniel was to see after in the morning. As for the rest of 'em – well, who do you favour, sir?'

At that moment there was a tap on the door. Justin called out permission and Selby entered. He tendered a note.

'Beg pardon, sir, but this message has just been delivered for you.'

Justin took the note and dismissed Selby. He tore it open, quickly mastering the contents.

'Lady Quainton desires me to wait on her urgently,' he told Watts. 'She adds that it concerns JK – I take that to mean Lady Kinver.'

'Tell you what, guv'nor,' said Watts excitedly. 'D'you suppose the lady's had another blackmail demand, same as Cleveland? You did say it was about time for one.'

Justin nodded. 'Precisely. You may as well accompany me, Joe, for I don't intend to stay long and we'll need to confer again afterwards.'

The visit was as brief as Justin had intended; but Lady Quainton omitted nothing of what she had learned from her friend, including the latter's conversation with Dr Wetherby.

'I must say it sounded very odd to me,' remarked Lady Quainton. 'Almost as if – but there, doubtless you'll know what to make of it. And you may as well have this,' – handing him the blackmail demand – 'for I must tell you that Jane is quite determined to post off the money at once, whatever you may advise to the contrary. I tried to persuade her to wait until I'd consulted you on that head but she simply refused to listen to reason. Poor dear, she is so petrified that the scandal will come to the light of day and who can blame her? Justin, you will do your possible to conceal the truth, should you unmask this villain? Which, of course, I am confident you *will* do, for I dare say you've quite decided already who it must be.'

'I'm grateful for your confidence, ma'am,' he said with a little mocking bow. 'But, yes, I have formulated a theory and now I hope to see it substantiated by proof. For Lady Kinver to dispatch the blackmail is the very thing to suit our purposes as then a watch can be kept at the receiving office.'

'Oh, yes!' she exclaimed, eagerly, 'and whoever collects that packet will be a self-confessed blackmailer! And Jane need not lose her money, for of course you'll have him arrested before he can do anything with it! What a good thing I didn't manage to dissuade her, after all.'

He agreed readily with this and having thanked her for her assistance took his leave.

Watts awaited him outside and soon they were back in Albemarle Street, comparing the two blackmail letters.

'Print from the *Gentleman's Magazine*, if I'm not mistaken,' pronounced Justin, studying both documents under a magnifying glass. 'That don't help, as it enjoys a wide circulation throughout the country. I wonder, though, how he disposed of the mutilated copies? Back of the fire, I suppose – easy enough, too.'

Watts evidently regarded these speculations as being beside the point.

'The thing is, sir, both these demands are for the same amount payable on the same day at the same office. That makes matters simpler for us. I'll look in and see the postmaster, make arrangements.'

'There must be nothing to set alarum bells ringing in our man's head,' warned Justin.

'Lord love us no, guv'nor! I ain't wet behind the ears,' protested Watts in a pained tone. 'Naught to frighten him off until he gets those packets in his bunch o' fives, and then – '

Justin nodded. 'There *is* a possibility of complications, though, so we'd best be prepared. We'll need another Runner, I think, Joe, and I'll remain on hand myself into the bargain.'

Chapter XVIII

*J*ustin had been quite right to distrust the gleam in his niece's eye when they had parted immediately before her short visit to the Bradfields' house in Sussex. Anthea was determined to ignore his warning and to do her utmost to discover anything which might have some bearing on the mysterious Thompson's identity. She had from the first seized upon the information passed on to her by Justin that Thompson was the name of Bradfield's land agent. She felt convinced that there must be some connection and that a part, at any rate, of the solution to the mystery must lie here in Sussex.

She soon realized that it would be impossible for her to conduct clandestine searches in a house with which she was totally unfamiliar and which, moreover, was full of servants. It seemed equally impossible to question Mr Thompson himself, a man whom she saw only once briefly when their host was driving them round the estate and who looked eminently respectable.

Instead she concentrated on listening attentively to any scraps of conversation which seemed to have the slightest bearing on what her uncle considered significant points. The only result of this was that she earned a totally undeserved reputation for being a good listener, something which would have astounded all her relatives.

She was due to return to Town with the other visitors on Thursday; by Wednesday afternoon she had learned nothing and was in what she herself would have described as a flat despair. Then it seemed that fate relented.

She was strolling in the gardens on her own soon after nuncheon, while the rest of the party were sitting indoors. It was one of those rare April days when at times the sun is almost at summer heat and she sat down upon a bench behind a tall, sheltering yew hedge in order to luxuriate in the unexpected warmth. Suddenly she heard voices from the other side of the hedge and identified them as belonging to her host and hostess.

'I wish you will not return to Town with the others tomorrow,' said Mrs Bradfield plaintively. 'Why cannot you stay here with the children and myself?'

'Oh, there are business affairs to be seen to, my love,' he answered vaguely. 'Besides, I might say the same to you. Why couldn't you be content to remain in Town a little longer, instead of cutting short your visit to dash back here before you'd scarce had a chance to sample the pleasures of the season? Now, come back with me tomorrow, pray do!'

'Oh, no, William! Leave the children so that they won't see either of us? That would be monstrous – it would have the most deleterious effect on their development!'

'You're too anxious, my love. I seldom saw my own parents for more than an hour or so for weeks at a time when I was the same age as our brats, aye, and older,' he said cheerfully. 'And I can't discover that it's done me much harm, can you? Be truthful, now!'

'How can one tell? Such matters often do not appear for many years,' she replied in an obstinate tone. 'Only consider how dreadful it would be if our dear little Jack were to turn out like poor Thompson's son, for example!'

Anthea's attention had been imperfectly fixed up to this point and she had been on the verge of making her presence known; but now it suddenly sharpened at mention of that name.

Bradfield laughed shortly. 'No fear of that, Anna, my dear. The fact is that young Giles Thompson was always a bad hat from the start. What's more, far from neglecting him, his parents did their possible to give him every advantage in life. A gentleman's education – he was tutored by the same cleric who performed the office for me eight years previously – then Tonbridge School and Cambridge. He absconded from the university with a large sum which someone had been fool enough to leave within his reach and was never heard of again.'

'I thought you told me that the son had joined a troupe of

strolling players?'

'Yes, that was the last his parents heard and even then they knew nothing of the troupe or of their son's whereabouts. Even his mother's death didn't bring the fellow back here, so obviously he has cut all connections with his past. A good riddance, I'd say. But as to one of ours turning out the same because they don't see enough of me – well, gammon, my love! I dare say they're all the better for a little healthy neglect until they're old enough to enjoy a day's sport, y'know. They'll need a father's guiding hand then, perhaps.'

'Oh, William, there's no doing anything with you!' protested his wife. 'But we'd best join our visitors and think up some scheme for their entertainment this afternoon.'

The voices receded and Anthea waited only a few minutes before herself returning to the house.

That same morning, Justin and Runner Watts met in Lincoln's Inn Fields and strolled together for a time in the bright sunshine.

'All's settled with the postmaster, sir,' said Watts. 'A hidey-hole for me where I'll see a sign from the clerk when our man asks for the packets. Grimshaw hanging about outside, making out he's touting for a hackney coachman, and you, sir – where'll you be waiting?'

'The print shop next door,' said Justin promptly. 'There's enough scurrilous material there to keep me busy for a week, though I hope our man don't intend to be as long as that before he collects. A sign from Grimshaw will alert me. I'll keep near the window myself or else set the proprietor on to keep watch for me. That's all arranged. What news of our friend Cleveland?'

'He's dispatched the packet all right and tight. We've been careful to keep away from his house, as you suggested, in case anyone should be spying on him. Nor has he come to Bow Street. Sir Nathaniel met him instead in one of the clubs. Seems he's handed in his resignation – says he's finished and I don't doubt he is. Don't think the Stock Exchange intend a prosecution, though.'

149

'Well, at least he won't end up in the King's Bench prison like Cochrane. The best he can do is to flee to France as he intended when we stopped him.'

They had turned out of the Fields into Serle Street, making their way back to Chancery Lane, when a man passed by them, walking briskly. For a moment Justin caught a full view of his face and recognized it instantly.

This was the drunken actor who had knocked into him on the evening when he had been keeping watch on Dr Wetherby outside the Olympic Theatre.

He waited until the man had gone ahead a safe distance, then whispered this information to Watts.

'Let's see where he goes – maybe he lodges round here.'

Watts nodded. He could see no particular point in ascertaining where this man lived; but he seldom questioned the captain's decisions, experience having taught him that there was usually method in the other's seeming madness.

They sauntered aimlessly behind their quarry, following him the short distance along Serle Street and into Carey Street. After a few yards he halted and knocked upon one of the doors. It opened at once as though the occupant had been watching at the window for his arrival. A young girl stood on the doorstep, neat and trim in a muslin gown with pink ribbons, and with an inviting, provocative smile on her red lips. She vanished quickly as the visitor stepped inside, drawing the door to behind him.

The two in the street continued on their way without a backward glance but with intrigued expressions.

'Now, I wonder?' mused Watts. 'That female, all done up as fancy as you please, wasn't no landlady by my reckoning. What d'you think, sir?'

'My experience of the species is admittedly limited,' said Justin. 'All the same, I'd have expected something broader in the beam and about twenty years older, I must admit.'

'Exactly, and that female wouldn't be a day above eighteen, if *I'm* any judge o' womenfolk.'

'Which, my dear chap, of course you are, indubitably,' grinned Justin.

'Y'know, sir, I'm thinking,' went on Watts, ignoring this

sally. 'That clerk Probert, at the lawyer's in Lincoln's Inn Fields, you recollect, guv'nor? He said he lived in Carey Street and had a young daughter who was a handful – always after the men or they were after her, don't make much difference. Might well be that same wench, don't you reckon? And as you say this actor fellow's a bit of a loose screw, by what the doorkeeper told you, why, those two might well come together – nothing more likely. Actors are on the loose all day, while Probert's stuck in his office not knowing what Miss gets up to. What d'you think, sir?'

'It sounds probable,' agreed Justin, 'but not particularly helpful as far as our own mystery is concerned. Still, who knows? It may fit somewhere into the puzzle.'

They parted presently, Justin returning to Albemarle Street. He had not been home very long when Selby knocked upon the door of the library.

'Beg pardon, Mr Rutherford,' he said apologetically. 'There's a Mrs Barton asking to see you. Shall I admit her, sir?'

'Mrs Barton?' For a moment Justin was at a loss. 'Do I know the lady?'

'Yes, so she says, though one can't precisely call her a lady, sir. More of an upper servant I would suppose,' said Selby, with all the sense of hierarchy of a gentleman's gentleman.

Justin smacked a hand against his head.

'Oh, yes, *that* Mrs Barton!' he exclaimed. 'By all means show her in.'

A few moments later Nurse Barton entered the room, sensibly attired in a dark blue walking dress covered by a warm spencer, and a sober bonnet.

'How d'you do, ma'am?' Justin greeted her affably. 'Pray be seated. Can I offer you any refreshment?'

'Nothing, thank you, Mr Rutherford,' she replied, taking the chair he indicated. 'I do apologize for intruding on you in this way, but there's something I think you should know. My lady thinks so, too, but she didn't feel well enough to come herself.'

'You've come from Lady Kinver?'

She nodded. 'That's right, sir. You see, I had to tell her – but I'd best explain how it was.'

He also nodded, keeping silent. Whatever Nurse Barton

151

wished to communicate to him she would do it best in her own way without interruptions.

'It was after you came to see me a week ago,' she began. 'I'd no notion until then that my poor lady had been paying blackmail all those years on Miss Maria's account – I couldn't have believed anyone would be such a monster! But once you said, sir, how you meant to find the villain, and it wouldn't lead to open scandal for my lady, I began puzzling my wits as to how I could help.'

She paused and Justin looked at her rather as a schoolmaster looks at a bright pupil who has momentarily faltered in giving an answer.

'Well, there seemed one way, though I didn't think my lady would approve of it – raking over dead coals, she'd say, and causing Miss Maria unhappiness. But why shouldn't she share a little in her mother's unhappiness, especially as it had all gone by long since and no harm could come of it as far as she's concerned? So I went down to her home in Sussex and told her how things were, then asked her straight out if she'd spoken the truth when she'd said that Captain Tilsworth had been her seducer.'

'And did she answer you?'

'Not at first but I soon put a stop to any of that nonsense,' replied Nurse Barton firmly. 'In the end she confessed it had been a lie and told me just how it was. There'd been several young men she'd been flirting with while she was in her aunt's house but all was open and above-board with them. There's no denying she was a flighty girl, Maria. But there was one who didn't come courting her openly, like the others. She was completely infatuated with him at the time and used to steal out to meet him by night and other such goings-on. Of course, that could only end one way, as you'll agree, sir.'

Justin nodded.

'Which it did,' finished Nurse Barton grimly. 'She told me the whole. He seduced her in August and they went on seeing each other until she returned home to London in September. By the middle of October she knew she was pregnant but was too frightened to say anything to her mother or to me. She wrote to the man though, and he said he couldn't help her, but suggested ways of getting rid of the baby. Not long afterwards she had news of Tilsworth's death and then her seducer writes to suggest she should put the blame on the captain if the worst happens and she has to give birth to the child.'

'As you remarked when first I interviewed you, dead men tell no tales,' remarked Justin dryly.

'Exactly so, sir. Well, after the miscarriage she wrote once again to this – this blackguard – telling him that all was well and she'd blamed the captain, and that no one knew of the pregnancy besides her mother, Dr Wetherby and myself. She never heard another word from him again, sir, which don't surprise me in the least, for a fine specimen he is, as anyone can tell! But by then she'd got over her infatuation for him and was ready to enjoy herself again, putting the past behind her. She was only seventeen, after all,' said Nurse Barton trying to make allowances.

'Yes, a very pretty villain,' said Justin grimly. 'But you haven't yet told me his name.'

She told him. He was not surprised.

Anthea returned home on the Thursday afternoon and straightaway urged her father to invite his brother over for dinner.

'Why are you so anxious to see Justin?' he demanded suspiciously. 'I trust you haven't been up to any of your mad starts while you've been away! He *did* promise me not to set you on to any of this investigation of his!'

'Neither did he,' said Anthea calmly. 'Oh, papa, what a to-do you make over nothing. Cannot I wish to see my uncle without any ulterior motive, other than natural family affection?'

'The straight answer to that is No, my girl,' replied her father with a chuckle. 'Not while there's a mystery for you to dabble your fingers in – I know you only too well. However, I'll send round a message.'

As Justin chanced to be at liberty that evening, he accepted the invitation. Anthea lost no time in acquainting him with the conversation she had overheard.

'Do you think it's of any help?' she asked doubtfully. 'Only it did seem to me that if this man is a bad hat – '

'Tut, tut, child,' he reproved, tongue in cheek. 'Where do you pick up these cant expressions?'

'From you,' she replied promptly. 'No, seriously, Justin, they say he's a scoundrel and his name *is* Thompson – I feel most strongly that there must be some connection!'

'Yes,' he said thoughtfully, 'you may be right. Well, I'm an Oxford man myself, but I do possess a few friends who went to the other place. It may seem ungrateful but I think perhaps I shall tear myself away from Edward's splendid hospitality and do a round of the clubs in search of them.'

Chapter XIX

When Joseph Watts arrived unostentatiously at the receiving office in Fleet Street on Friday he was informed that the two packets for Mr Thompson were already there awaiting collection. Although the arrangements for surveillance were put into effect on the due date given by the blackmailer, no one expected that he would call that very day to collect his booty. The watchers were quite prepared to be obliged to wait several days – possibly even a week or more – before he did arrive. Justin in particular found this a melancholy prospect but acknowledged that there was no other way if he wished to see the affair through to its climax personally, rather than leave it in the hands of Bow Street. And this he was determined to do. He now knew the true identity of the blackmailer and Yarnton's murderer; but proof could only be provided by catching the culprit with those packets in his possession.

Throughout Friday and Saturday all three watchers remained at their posts until the receiving office closed for the night. During the hours of darkness and all day Sunday, another runner was on duty in case the blackmailer should decide to break into the office and take his packets by a less orthodox method. This was not likely, as the ensuing hue and cry would be the last thing he desired, but it was a possibility they could not afford to overlook.

By the time Monday afternoon came round Justin was chafing at the delay. The print shop where he was taking cover provided ample entertainment in the way of caricatures satirizing the London scene, but after two days spent in studying these he found their possibilities exhausted. He indulged in a mild grumble when he slipped in to see Watts briefly from time to time, making use of the rear doors of both premises, which were well away from public view.

'Bless you, sir, we're used to it,' was all the consolation Watts could offer. 'Most cases involve us in surveillance, sometimes for just a few hours, but other times for weeks on end. But if you'd prefer Bow Street to take over – '

'Good God no, Joe! You don't think I've spent so much time on this affair to cry craven at the last ditch? Perish the thought!'

It was during one of these intervals when they were together that a signal was passed to Watts that someone had arrived in the office asking for Mr Thompson's post.

'But it's a female, Mr Watts,' whispered the postmaster, drawing the runner to the spyhole which afforded a good view of the counter. 'Over there, see, a pretty young girl. The clerk's making a business of handing the packets over, awaiting your orders.'

Justin also took a look. He and Watts eyed each other, then nodded.

'Wench we saw t'other day with that actor chap,' said Watts in a low tone. 'Shall we arrest her now, sir, or wait and see what she does with 'em?'

'Wait, decidedly. She's not the culprit, only a messenger. We'll follow her and she should lead us to him. Warn Grimshaw – best have him along as well.'

The girl was handed the packets, which she stowed away in a basket she was carrying, then left the receiving office. People were constantly coming and going, both in the office itself and in the street outside; so she paid not the slightest heed to the three men who followed close on her heels as she continued along Fleet Street and into Chancery Lane. Presently she turned into Carey Street.

'She's taking 'em to her home,' muttered Watts. 'He may be waiting there.'

Justin nodded and quickly instructed Grimshaw to make his way to the rear of the house where the girl lived to keep a look out for anyone trying to escape that way. Meanwhile he and Watts continued past the house until they saw the girl enter, then turned back smartly and knocked on the door.

She opened it at once, the basket still on her arm. At the sight of two total strangers on the doorstep her eyes widened in

156

surprise. Before she could collect herself, Watts displayed the crown on his official baton.

'A word with you in private, miss.'

She stared at the baton, seeming not to understand.

'The law, miss,' explained Watts. 'Now will you let us in?'

'Oh!'

She certainly sounded surprised, but neither guilty nor afraid, as Justin noticed. She set down the basket, opened the door wider to admit them both, then shut it and stood regarding them in a puzzled way.

'Miss Probert, I believe?' asked Justin.

'Yes, I'm Kitty Probert – but how d'you know me? And who are you?'

'Is there anyone else in the house, miss?' asked Watts, looking suspiciously about him.

'No, there's no one here at present. What d'you want with me? There's naught wrong is there? My pa – '

'Be easy, Miss Probert,' said Justin soothingly. 'Your parent's pursuing his lawful occasions at the offices of Binns & Moody, as usual. Our business is with your good self.'

'With *me?*' Amazement brought a squeak to her voice. 'What can you want with me?'

'Perhaps we might sit down somewhere for a few moments,' suggested Justin, still in the same gentle tone, 'so that we can explain.'

'Oh, yes, of course.'

She picked up her basket, leading the way into a room off the hall at the rear of the house. Through the window Watts caught a glimpse of his colleague lurking in the small backyard.

'Sit down, do,' she invited, setting the basket down on a small table. 'Now, what in the world is this all about, pray?'

'There are two postal packets in yon basket, miss,' said Watts, nodding his head towards the article in question. 'You just picked them up from the office in Fleet Street – that's so?'

'Well, yes – ' she agreed, hesitantly.

'The name written on them is Mr Thompson,' continued Watts. 'Right again?'

She nodded silently.

'Just what d'ye intend to do with them there packets? Keep

157

'em?'

'Oh, no, no! I collected them for a friend. There's naught wrong with that, is there?'

'Depends,' answered Watts laconically. 'What's the name of this friend?'

She gave them a coy glance.

'Come, now, gennelmen, you can't expect a girl to give away all her secrets.'

'No, only this one,' said Watts. 'Cut the cackle, m'dear, and come to the 'osses. Who is he?'

'Does it matter? Oh, very well,' – as she saw the Runner tighten his mouth – 'no harm in telling you as long as you don't go and let on to pa. You won't do that, will you?' she added in consternation.

'Have no fear,' Justin assured her. 'Tell me, have you often performed this service for your friend?'

Instinctively she reacted to his careless charm and air of Quality. She fluttered her eyelashes and gave him a provocative glance.

'Oh, yes, two or three times altogether.'

'His name,' grated Watts.

She turned a petulant look upon him but at sight of his grim face she quickly replied. 'Mr Treherne – Theobald Treherne.'

'Then how come these packets are directed to a Mr Thompson?'

'Truth to tell I don't know, nor never thought to ask,' she said somewhat tartly. 'When he comes to see me, we've better things to talk about.'

'I'll wager any odds on that,' put in Watts.

She gave him an indignant look. 'There's no call to take that tone with me – I ain't a criminal, I'll have you know! I just did him a favour by collecting his mail as anyone might do. I'm sure I never heard so much fuss about a couple of letters in my life!'

'Are you expecting Mr Treherne to call on you presently?' asked Justin quietly.

'If you must know I am,' she said, glancing at the clock, 'so I'd be obliged if you'd leave.'

'Not so fast, young woman.' Watts moved close up to her so

that she flinched away from him. 'We're not going anywheres – leastways, not until we set eyes on your Mr Treherne and have a few words with him.'

'Oh, no!' she cried in dismay. 'Why can't you leave us alone? We've done no harm that I know of!'

'That's just it – there's a whole heap you don't know yet, missie. Now, listen to me. When's this cully likely to arrive here?'

'In about a quarter hour,' she answered sulkily.

'Then we'll wait. And when he comes to the door, mind you let him in without tipping him the wink. I'll be right behind you, just to make sure as you remember,' he warned her.

For the first time she looked frightened. She glanced from one to the other of the two men realizing that she was in their power. It was not a pleasant thought, even though they represented the forces of law and order.

'What do you mean to do to him?' she whispered.

'Ask him a few questions – perhaps take him in to Bow Street,' replied Watts.

She shivered, subsiding into a chair.

'How long have you known this man?' demanded Watts.

'Something over six months, I suppose.'

'And I collect your father isn't aware of the association?' put in Justin.

She shook her head vigorously. 'No, he'd get into a rare frenzy if he knew I was seeing any gennelman on the quiet. He reckons I should bring them home for him to look over and approve,' she answered petulantly.

'An absurd notion of course,' said Justin.

She looked at him suspiciously but he kept a straight face.

'Well, so it is, whatever you may think, sir! We just chanced to be walking in the Fields – Lincoln's Inn, y'know – one afternoon, and fell into conversation. Where's the harm in that, in broad daylight, I'd like to know? Of course, it don't do for pa, so I says nothing to him. Mr Treherne is an actor so he's at liberty in the daytime and often feels the need of a bit o' company, like I do myself.'

'So you became friends and invited him to your home? And then he asked you to collect his mail?'

She nodded. 'And where's the harm in that, I'd like to know?' She broke off as the door knocker sounded. 'There he is now!'

'Steady on,' warned Watts as she hastened to the door. 'Remember – not a word to him – just let him in and I'll do the rest.'

He followed at her heels as she went through the hall and opened the front door, standing just behind it as the man entered.

As she closed the door the visitor at once gathered her into his arms but she pushed him away.

'What's the matter?' he demanded, trying to seize her again.

It was then that he saw Watts. His face changed as he turned on her accusingly.

'And who's this, pray? B'God, if you've been playing me false, madam – '

'It's the law – Bow Street Runner – '

He stood stock still, his face paling.

'Mr Theobald Treherne?' said Watts. 'A word with you, sir, if you please. In here.'

He indicated the room where Justin was still waiting, now on his feet. All three entered, Treherne looking warily at the other two men.

'What do you want with me?' he asked.

'First of all, to know your real name,' said Watts.

'What's wrong with Theobald Treherne?' asked the actor in a would-be defiant tone.

'Nothing – on the boards,' replied Justin, surveying him through his quizzing glass. 'An excellent name for that purpose I would say. But we have reason to believe, my dear sir, that you began life under a much more commonplace moniker – shall we say that of Giles Thompson?'

'Fustian! I never heard such nonsense – you're making a mistake – '

'I think not,' said Justin quietly. 'This young lady has some packets addressed to Mr Thompson which she informs us she means to hand over to you. Therefore, your real name is Thompson.'

'No, no! I can explain all that – '

'Tell it to the magistrate,' advised Watts in a grim manner.

'I'm arresting you, Giles Thompson, alias Theobald Treherne, on a charge of blackmail and also of the murder of Marmaduke Yarnton – '

'*What!*' Treherne's face was as white as Miss Probert's dimity curtains. 'I tell you I know naught about blackmail or, or – *murder!* As for that name – what did you say it was? – I never set eyes on its owner in my life!'

'Then how do you account for these?' demanded Watts, striding over to Kitty Probert's basket and abstracting the two postal packets from it.

'I – oh, God!' Treherne sank on to a chair. 'Whatever I say, you're not going to believe me!'

'Then let us not strain your powers of invention,' said Justin. 'We know you are Giles Thompson, son of a respectable man who is employed as an agent on the estate of Mr Bradfield in Sussex. Do you deny this? I warn you, we can bring proof.'

'Yes – I mean to say – oh, what the devil's the use? Yes, my real name is Thompson, but if you think I've aught to do with murder, you much mistake the matter! As for blackmail, the boot's on the other foot!'

'Ah!' Justin exclaimed in satisfaction. 'You would say that someone is blackmailing you?'

The other nodded, seemed about to speak, then compressed his lips.

'About four years ago, you were an undergraduate at Cambridge, were you not? You left hurriedly, I understand, taking with you a sum of money not belonging to you – no doubt an oversight but these things are readily misunderstood,' continued Justin smoothly. 'Bow Street were alerted and sought you for a time without success. You had been discreet, cutting off all communication with family and associates and joining a small band of travelling players who were moving about constantly in the northern parts of the country. Later, when the hue and cry had died down, you came south using your pseudonym of Theobald Treherne, and sought employment in the London playhouses. This is accurate, is it not?'

'Yes, damn you, yes!' groaned Thompson.

'So far, so good. And now perhaps you will explain these postal packets. They are directed to you, collected for you by

161

Miss Probert, and you are here in person to receive them. We know for a fact that they contain money extorted by a black-mailer. Do you intend to deny that you are the person responsible?'

'Yes – yes – I do – you've got to believe me!' Thompson said shakily. 'What you've said about my past, that's true enough, but not this other business, as God's my judge! I tell you, those packets are naught to do with me – I collect them for someone else! Someone who saw me in a performance about a year since, recognized me as Thompson and knew about the Cambridge affair! He threatened to give me away unless I did this for him – paid me for it too, which was more than I expected, and mighty useful for times have been hard lately! I know it sounds an unlikely story but it's true, so help me! You've *got* to believe me!'

'This man's name?' demanded Justin.

Thompson shook his head.

'I don't know who he is, I swear it! He sends me anonymous letters made up out of newsprint, telling me when and where to collect his post and making appointments for me to hand it over to him.'

'Then you've met him,' accused Watts, 'so you'd recognize him at any rate.'

'Not so. He meets me in some quiet spot after dark. He's always muffled up in a cloak with his face concealed by a mask. He never stays more than a minute or so and don't speak more than a few words. I've tried to puzzle out who he may be, but damned if I can succeed – not that it would do me any good if I did know,' he added with a shudder. 'I've no fancy to try turning the tables on him, for I reckon he could be an ugly customer.'

'In that you're correct,' said Justin, 'as he's already murdered one man who guessed his identity. It may reassure you to hear that we believe what you've told us, Thompson. And now you're about to assist us in bringing this villain to justice. When and where are you to meet him?'

*

Shortly after the interval in the performance at the Olympic

Theatre that evening a carriage drew up and a gentleman alighted, entering by the stage door. He was at once recognized by the doorkeeper, who greeted him cordially.

'You're early tonight, y'r honour. D'ye wish to go straight along to Miss Nympsfield's dressing-room or would ye rather see the rest of the performance?'

Miss Nympsfield's gentleman friend indicated his preference for going backstage, pressed a coin into a willing palm and proceeded on his way. Few people were about as most were busy with their accustomed tasks; but he noticed in passing one of the minor actors, usually to be observed in a drunken fuddle when not onstage, but now unusually sober and looking a trifle unwell. The gentleman smiled sardonically to himself as he pushed open the somewhat dilapidated door of his lady love's sanctum.

Justin Rutherford was also visiting the Olympic that evening. He arrived just before the interval, intending to employ that period of light and movement in looking about him. He had no wish to become caught up in conversation with anyone he knew, however, so kept his distance when he saw a group of Velmond's friends, Bradfield amongst them, strolling about in the passage behind the row of boxes.

After the lights had dimmed he made his way quietly out of the theatre and round to the rear, where there was a small open courtyard, unlit save for a lantern hanging beside a door used only by workmen. The angles of the building afforded a certain amount of cover and the night was dark, the moon being obscured by cloud. Justin glided stealthily round the building, pausing at the two points where Watts and Grimshaw were stationed to exchange a few words with each before concealing himself close by.

A nearby clock chimed nine. The workmen's door opened and Theobald Treherne, alias Thompson, emerged hesitantly into the light of the lamp. He stood there silently, not attempting to search out the other men concealed in the courtyard.

Time passed; the clock sounded the quarter hour. Immediately afterwards a dark figure, only just discernible in the gloom, stepped out of the alleyway into the courtyard and advanced towards the waiting actor.

He stopped well short of the lamp but close enough to make himself heard without shouting.

'You've got them?' he asked hoarsely.

Thompson nodded, holding up the packets to the light.

'Bring them here,' commanded the other.

Thompson slowly walked the few yards between himself and the other man, then handed over the packets with trembling fingers.

The masked man stowed them quickly away but no sooner had he done so than running footsteps sounded behind him and the heavy hand of Watts came down on his shoulder.

'I arrest you in the name o' the law!'

With a violent jerk the man shook himself free and turned, producing a pair of pistols from the pockets of his cloak. He levelled them at Watts and Grimshaw, who had joined his colleague.

'Stand or I fire!' he warned.

'I shouldn't, if I was you,' countered Watts. 'Now just you come along quiet like – '

The masked man made no answer but began to back away towards the alley, still keeping the two Runners covered. Perforce they froze in their tracks.

Suddenly Thompson, who had been likewise standing motionless, sank half fainting to the ground. Mistaking his intentions the masked man fired at him.

'Down – get down!'

Justin's shouted command to the Runners came at the same moment as he launched himself upon their opponent. Surprised by an attack from that quarter the masked man spun round and fired his second pistol.

He had no time to take proper aim so the ball went wide.

Flinging aside his now useless pistols, the masked man tried to make a run for it. But the odds were against him and soon he lay spreadeagled on the ground, knocked senseless by Justin's punishing right.

Justin ripped away the mask, though he knew very well whose face would be revealed.

It was that of Roderick Peyton.

Chapter XX

I must say I'm relieved to know that this diabolical affair has been resolved at last,' remarked Lord Rutherford to his brother when they met several days later. 'You say Peyton's confessed to Yarnton's murder and that the blackmail victims need have not the slightest fear of anything coming to light as far as they are concerned. I'm sure they have much for which to thank you, as I don't doubt it's largely due to your efforts on their behalf.'

'Fustian! It was a highly successful combined effort on the part of my accomplices, not the least of these being your own daughter, old fellow. Had it not been for Anthea's assistance, I should never have discovered that blackmail was the root of the motive for Yarnton's murder.'

'Ah, well, possibly you consider I should feel flattered by that, but devil a bit! That girl's too resty by half, Justin – I'll never know an easy moment until she's wed and some other poor devil is responsible for her freakish starts.'

'You can't gammon me,' grinned Justin. 'You're as proud as a peacock of the chit if you own the truth.'

'Oh, well, possibly so. But look here, Justin, there are still a good many things I don't understand about this affair of Yarnton's murder and I warn you that Anthea's sure to be pestering the life out of one of us to know the whole, so you may as well explain it to me.'

'Yes, indeed, for I'm afraid she'll need an expurgated version. Some of the details are scarce suitable for the ears of a delicately nurtured female.'

'You must be thinking of someone else, my dear chap! Anthea ain't delicately nurtured – mean to say, we did our best of course, but it just didn't take,' complained Edward. 'But let's hear a full account of Peyton's intrigues. How did the villain come by his information? It's easy enough to see that as Cleveland's secretary he would have access to incriminating documents concerning his employer, but what of the other two, poor Lady Kinver and little Lucy Velmond?'

'Lady Kinver's involvement began in 1810 when Peyton was eighteen and living at home in Buckinghamshire waiting to go up to Cambridge in the autumn. He was bored by his family, so consoled himself with the local females, always being in the petticoat line. Quite by chance he met Maria Kinver, who was spending the summer with an aunt in the neighbourhood. Maria was only seventeen and a bit of a minx. The aunt allowed her too much freedom, so before long she was conducting flirtations with every young man thereabouts. These were all quite open but the affair with Peyton was otherwise, doubtless at his instigation. The two met secretly several times and before long the inevitable happened and he had seduced her.'

Edward whistled. 'With, I collect, dire results?'

Justin nodded. 'She discovered that she was pregnant after she'd returned to Town to her parents. By this time Peyton was at Cambridge. She wrote to him but the only help he offered was to suggest ways in which she might induce an abortion. She realized that marriage with him was out of the question, even had he suggested it, because of his youth and lack of money. She was too frightened to confide in her mother so she muddled on, hoping matters would right themselves.'

'Poor child!' said Edward compassionately. 'She may have been foolish but one feels for her.'

'Indeed. At the end of October, both Maria and Peyton heard, through separate sources, of the death in the Peninsular war of a certain Captain Tilsworth, who'd been Maria's most serious suitor during her stay in Buckinghamshire. He'd been home on furlough at the time. Peyton wrote suggesting that if matters came to the worst she should put the blame for her condition on the dead man – a sound enough scheme and worthy of Peyton, one feels.' Edward nodded grimly. 'Whether she took any means to bring it about, I can't say, but at the end of November she suffered a miscarriage. Three people were obliged to know then – Lady Kinver, Dr Wetherby, who attended her, and the girl's nurse. Maria named the captain as her seducer. Only the nurse, who had known Maria since babyhood, was not convinced that she was telling the truth. Recently, when I interviewed Nurse Barton during the course of my investigations, she expressed these doubts to me. Later she went to Maria Wingrave's home in Sussex to confront her. She discovered the truth and brought the information to me. It was the last link in my chain of evidence, although by then I'd already guessed how it must have been.'

'Diabolical!' exploded Edward. 'D'you mean to say this villain not only seduced the girl but later blackmailed her mother on that account? Of all the cold-blooded, venomous – ' He broke off, too irate to conclude the sentence.

'Words do fail one, I agree,' said Justin. 'It was not so very much later that he began the blackmail, either – it was soon after Maria's wedding in 1811. Twice-yearly demands have been arriving ever since. My attention was caught from the first by the fact that the early payments were to be directed to offices roughly north of London, whereas for the past two years London offices have been stated. No doubt this was because Peyton came down from Cambridge in 1813 and became Cleveland's secretary, so was domiciled in London. He began blackmailing his employer in the following year, using the same methods as for Lady Kinver and demanding the same amount in payment.'

'And I suppose he found out about poor little Lucy Velmond from Cleveland's daughter?'

'Yes, I collect Mrs Cleveland was quite anxious at one time about her daughter's friendship with the secretary. No doubt Lucy's secret was divulged during that period. I don't know what it may be but I believe Anthea does.'

'Tell me, Justin, why did the villain use the name Thompson for this blackmail business? I know you said it was the real name of that poor actor chap whom Peyton shot when the Runners arrested him, but what was the connection between them?'

'They were both at Cambridge at the same time and therefore Peyton knew all about Thompson's disgrace and subsequent flight. When he needed a pseudonym for his blackmailing activities, he adopted that of Thompson – perhaps by a process of association. That wasn't the end of it. About a year ago Peyton recognized Thompson in the guise of a down-at-heel actor calling himself Theobald Treherne. Having already established a pattern of blackmail, he used the same method to coerce Thompson into collecting the packets from various receiving offices. And I'm tolerably certain,' added Justin, 'that it was Thompson who ransacked Yarnton's rooms and later hired the ruffians who set upon Watts and myself.

'There was a snuff box missing from Yarnton's place – the Runners had taken an inventory just after the murder – and we found it on Thompson's dead body.'

'What about Dr Wetherby? I know you had suspicions of him at one time.'

'Yes, I certainly gained the impression that he knew something when first I asked him about the name Thompson. He did, of course, not only about the Kinver scandal but also about the blackmail. I've taxed him with this since Peyton's arrest and he's admitted that he once caught sight of a blackmail demand when he was visiting Lady Kinver professionally. His view was that nothing could be done to bring the blackmailer to book without causing extreme distress to both Lady Kinver and her daughter, so it was best for her to continue paying.'

'Something in that, I suppose, and she's a wealthy woman of course. Not that I can entirely agree with him. Ah, well, my dear boy, you'll be free now to follow up your own interests. I suppose you'll be solving the mysteries of some ancient tomb next?'

'George, there is something I must tell you,' said Lucy Velmond with an air of decision which belied her quaking inner feelings.

Velmond had been giving her an account of the Peyton affair, having just returned from a session with Justin Rutherford in his rooms.

He smiled fondly and put an arm about her. She removed it gently but firmly.

'No – wait until you have heard me,' she went on.

He gave her a keen look. 'You sound vastly serious, my love.'

168

'I am. I don't know how to tell you, George – indeed, I would have done so before this if only I could have summoned up the courage – '

'Courage?' He frowned. 'You alarm me, Lucy – speak out! There isn't – there isn't anyone else, is there?'

'No, no! Never – there never could be! But there's something you should know about me – a secret from my past. You know you were saying that – that odious villain Peyton was blackmailing Mr Cleveland and a lady whose name was not revealed? Well,' she went on desperately, 'he was also blackmailing *me*.'

Velmond stared at her, thunderstruck. '*You*! I don't believe it!'

She nodded miserably. 'It's true, alas. He had discovered that I was in disgrace some years ago, when I was at school – in fact I was *expelled*, George!'

'Oh, yes, but – '

She put her hand over his lips. 'No, pray let me finish now I've begun, dearest! You see, it was like this. There was to be a gala night at the Sydney Gardens – I was at school in Bath, you know – and all the girls were quite wild to attend. But, of course, it was strictly forbidden. Then the dancing master said that he would take a few of us surreptitiously, if we could manage to creep out after lights out in the dormitory and meet him in the school garden by the rear entrance. I wouldn't have done it – I am not bold by nature! – but my friend Selina was quite otherwise and determined to go. She said it would be selfish of me not to join her as she couldn't go alone with Monsieur Ricard. So I steeled myself to make the attempt.'

'My poor darling!' She saw his shoulders were shaking and could not decide why.

'But she played me false,' continued Lucy indignantly. 'She came only as far as the back door of the building, then told me to go on and she would follow in a few minutes, as she'd forgotten to bring something or other. I believed her – why should I not? I did as she bid me and joined Monsieur Ricard by the gate. She never came but the headmistress did! Oh, George, I shall never forget the shame! So I was expelled and my father was extremely angry – as I'm sure he had every right

169

to be. It was hushed up and after that I was very strictly guarded at home. But naturally Cecilia Cleveland knew of it, as we were at school together, and I see now that the blackmailer would have discovered my secret by that means. Oh, George, when the demand came, I *dare not* tell you! And so I pawned my mother's necklace to raise the money and then had to tell you a tissue of lies to account for my being in a dubious quarter alone – which that horrid man Yarnton revealed to Lady Quainton and you overheard! Oh, George, can you ever, *ever* forgive me for any of it? Do not say that I have forfeited your love and trust for ever!'

He gathered her into his arms and demonstrated convincingly that he had no intention of saying anything of the kind. After an interval he held her a little away from him, surveying her with a quizzical smile.

'My sweetest life, you could have saved yourself all the agony of concealment,' he said gently. 'That scapegrace brother of yours told me your secret some time since.'

'Oh! If that isn't just like him! And papa said that it must never be mentioned to anyone!'

'A suitable parental attitude, no doubt, but most men think nothing of a mere schoolgirl scrape, especially such an innocent one. I don't propose to give it another thought, except to recover your necklace for you.'

'It really doesn't matter, dearest,' murmured Lucy into his coat, to which she found herself once again pressed. 'It's the most hideous thing!'